I Met Your Husband Last Night

"Saving
One Wife
At A Time"

April de Cardenas

Published By:
Sebi Publishing Group, Inc.
New York

Written By:
April de Cardenas

This is a work of fiction. Resemblances of names, places, stories and events are solely from the imagination of the author. In general terms, everything is made up.

ISBN 978-0-615-23411-3

Edition II, Volume I

Library of Congress Control Number: 2009907532

Cover Photography
John Bailey ©

Cover Models
Laureta Meci and Jason Rosselli

PRINTED IN THE UNITED STATES
WGA Number 1373335

Special Thanks:

To Jules my adorable husband, thank you for being crazy enough to marry me, tolerate my imagination and allowing me to have clicker control for the sake of our marriage.

To my six children, I thank all of you for letting Mommy type, not questioning why Mom is laughing when writing and for understanding none of you can read this book until you are of legal age, but certainly before you get married!

Thank you to all of my friends and family for supporting me, giggling over these stories and never forgetting to bring the wine.

And finally to all of those husbands who finally had me say enough is enough. This book is my Thank You to all of you. Your secret is out and I'm sending your wife a copy. (Smiles)

April de Cardenas

Saving One Wife at a Time. A married woman discovers her husband had been cheating on her. When she recovers from her broken heart, she decides to help out all of the other unsuspecting wives. Putting on her stilettos as a super hero puts on a cape; she heads into the evening to have chance encounters with married men. After the night is over, she drafts a letter of the husband's behavior and mails it to his wife. Dear Christy, I Met Your Husband Last Night! The book is filled with different letters and journal entries. It was not written for the faint at heart as it contains adult sexual content and situations. *Expected to be a National Best Seller and every husband's worst nightmare.*

THE PROMISE

I, "Ted", take "You" to be my lawfully wedded wife, my best friend, my <u>faithful partner</u> from this day forward until the end of time. In the presence of God, our family and close friends, I offer you my devotional vow to be your faithful partner in sickness and in health, in good times and in bad, and in joy as well as in sorrow. I promise to always love you unconditionally, to trust you and our bond, to honor and respect you, to laugh with you and cry with you, and to cherish you for as long as we both shall live. You are my one and only love. Nothing can or will ever come between us.

THE PERFECT MARRIAGE

The rain started out softly on my window, making soothing sounds escalating me further into peacefulness. Lights flashed through the sky illuminating the naked silhouette beside me. I admired him through my eyes filled with all the love in the world.

The storm started moving more in our direction; the drops became heavier beating in rhythm with my lover's breathing. The thunder and lightning would clash without warning, causing me to jump in surprise. Taking advantage of the vulnerable feeling I had within, I cuddled closer to my husband in our warm bed. Ted's strength, even though he was sleeping, calmed me. I was safe and secure within his arms. Everything was just right. I had the perfect marriage.

Anytime I was this close to my husband, a ping of passion would stir between my legs. The attraction which I felt for him was overwhelming at times. Ted was my first and only love. Medical journals will say women become more sexual as they get older. I will agree with that analogy. The libido is a powerful asset of any female and it seems only fitting it would become stronger as we learn to accept our bodies as the masterpieces they are.

Almost at suddenly as it came, the weather moved away from us. My husband was still sleeping as I continued to become more excited with the prospect of desire. Moving my hands across his naked chest, I wondered if I could get him aroused while he was sleeping without actually waking him up.

My desire had become a full blown case of a hormonal appetite which needed to be satisfied. Thinking my little plan should not be too hard to accomplish. Ted did sleep naked, I slipped my hands under the covers and touched him. I was gentle at first. He moved a little, his breathing picked up a little and slowly, he grew. I can't express how hot it was to do this to him while he was unconscious, an erotic new adventure for a couple who has been married for five years. Our relationship was always great because we were both happy with our jobs and decided to hold off on having any children. No need to fight about money or kids.

Continuing to massage my toy, I finally slid on top of him. I was drenched and easily able to take him inside of me without using my hands. He moaned but never opened his eyes. With a husky morning voice he said to me "Oh God, Gloria, that feels so good." And I replied "Who's Gloria?"

Ouch.

REALITY BITES

Dear Reader,

My life forever changed at the moment of discovery. My husband was cheating on me. I was devastated. How could I be so blind and stupid?

Some wives want to blame the girlfriend; I quickly overcame that ridiculous train of thought. The responsibility was my husbands. Ted was the inhuman idiot who had no regard for me, our relationship or the five years I had given him. He took our marriage and flushed in down the toilet, pausing long enough to wash his hands so he would not get caught. But he did get busted.

It wasn't just my relationship which was broken, I was shattered. Better put, I was a mess. Perfect became ugly.

So what happened? I divorced Ted, took my fifty percent, cried for two years and remained numb. I could no longer watch romantic movies. Seeing a loving couple made me want to puke. When the mailman delivered envelopes in Ted's name, I cursed under my breath every time. I even went so far as to get a voodoo doll. When feeling a little blue, stabbing my stuffed ex right in the groin with the sharp needle offered some satisfaction.

Life went on though; I would casually meet other men but most happened to already be involved or married. Their real names however could have been Steve, Joe or Dan, to me they were all "Ted the Bastard".

Every storm for a couple years was like a flashback. Each drop of rain which hit my glass was torture on me. I use to love rain. Then it occurred to me that showers wash away the old and promote and nurture the new. I quit trying to figure out what it was I did wrong, instead I started asking the Steves, Joes and Dans why they cheat and if their wives know it. It's amazing how much guys will blab. They want to tell someone, so they tell me.

Reaching the conclusion that many men are born to breed, I moved forward.

If we analyze history, it was man's job to populate earth. God created them with an endless amount of sperm cells. On the other hand, women are born with a predefined amount of eggs (which also happen to expire. Where is the equality in that?)

Could it be that this endless amount of swimmers has caused this epidemic? Even if they are getting it at home, they still can't help themselves when tempted by a woman.

After recuperating from the shock of infidelity and the "new age" dating scene, I decided to make it my life's mission to save as many of the wives I can. There is, of course, dual pleasure in this for me sometimes. I help out the women and get satisfied at the same time, either sexually or in a heroic way.

Someone's husband is out fooling around on them. Living two live's and spoiling the other woman. Poor wifey, sitting there after all of those years, having to pick old fruit from the same tree. What once were plump juicy plums are now only bitter shrunken wrinkled prunes. At least with her!

In the old days, even if the wife knew her husband was out messing around, she may have thought "Well, he only has a couple more years left that he can get it up". The medical industry has changed things for us. Men can now screw around until they drop in the grave.

Every night is an adventure for me. I am armed with my stilettos and a mission to beef up court filings or at least make the playing field even. I seek chance encounters with married men and then enlighten their wives with a personal mailed letter from me.

I have saved copies of every correspondence I have written so far. However, this method of spreading my message is taking too long. Over a really good bottle of red wine, I brainstormed my latest vessel to carry my word faster and further. I wrote this book.

Sure I could have just written a book about adultery, but I felt that sharing my letters and journal entries gives a better understanding that this can happen to anyone. This is your chance to peek behind closed doors. Maybe even your own front door.

If you are married and have never received a letter from me, then, as of this moment you are safe. The letters contained herein are just a small collection of experiences I have had with married men. Several of them have happy endings, others do not and then there are those so peculiar that you will be grateful to see the male described is not your husband or even your boyfriend!

Honestly, I was very surprised Ted would cheat me on. I am beautiful and sexy; every man's desire. I never doubted him for a minute. We had sex daily, I'm quite the acrobat in bed, and we each had some fetishes; acting on them together.

Truthfully I look forward to meeting that bitch who destroyed my marriage. No, I am not bitter anymore; she actually did me a favor! I have a high opinion of the word "Bitch", for that's one word men fear! I would only want to thank her for doing me a favor. Of course, I did not see it as a favor at the time.

Eventually, married women will be grateful to me. They may even find themselves sending out letters of their own. Just keep in mind if a woman remains married long enough, I will get around to her husband too. I promise to continue nailing those bastards and letting you know.

xoxo,
The Other Woman

Mission Statement: "Saving One Wife at a Time"

"The First Step After Recovery"

JOURNAL

Dear Diary,

It's been a long time since I shared my inner soul with you. Everyone told me I needed to see a shrink, someone to help me through my mourning period, a professional to guide me during those gloomy days to reach recovery.

Did it help? Maybe a little, but time does heal all wounds. It took just over two years for the hole in my heart to close. The opening was quite large; a 747 jet could pass through it without me noticing.

The final step of my treatment is to actually go on a date. It's been a long time; I am pretty nervous. I'm not sure I know how to do it anymore. It will be so strange to be with a guy who is not belching and farting at the dinner table.

I have been asked out many times but no one really interested me. The quickening of the heart, sweating of the palms, and difficulty speaking maybe only happen in movies. This is a new generation of dating and, of course, a new beginning for me, perhaps internet profiles may be a place to start.

Think about it. I get to go shopping for a date! I imagine it could resemble a football stadium. Announcing over the intercom…. "All single men please rise. Sit down if you are not in shape. Sit down if you are balding and refuse to just shave your head. Sit down if you are unemployed. Sit down if you are a mama's boy. Sit down if you do not have excellent hygiene, etc."

Of course many of those online ads will be bullshit. I mean who is really going to tell the truth.

So tonight, I begin my search for the perfect date.

SEARCH RESULTS

Morning Wood...who needs FUN? Handsome and Talented... - m4w - 42

Who can meet right now and give my 8.5 inch a good sucking? I'm willing to finger lick or do nothing but watch at your request. Handsome married professional working with dark hair, blue eyes, athletic body, really nice white teeth, tanned face and body. Really huge thick cock with a big thick head on it you have to see. If you want to see just to give it a hand job, you are welcome to do that as well.

Friend - Keep It A Secret! - m4w - 63

Hi, I am a 63 year old male and married looking for a lady between ages 30 to 80. Natural hard on, no medication. If there are any lonely married or single ladies who would like a good email friend. Also lady who would like nice massage or kissing and cuddling, send me email please.

Any Lactating Chicks? - m4w - 35

I would love to empty your sweet milk-laden breasts this morning or on any other day. I am a clean, discreet, well packed, DD-free married gentleman and expect the same. DESCRET is the key word. Not looking for sex, just your breasts.

Very Sexy Married Man - Curious About Giving Head -49

Good looking, smooth married man - sexy, 6 foot 2" tall - 183lbs - full blond hair - brown eyes - not looking for too much contact - just want to please a man orally - MUST BE SUPER CLEAN - married is a huge plus - DISCREET . DD free must wear condom.

MWM looking for... - m4w - 37

Looking for a night time fun. Married, wife works midnights and kids will be sleeping. Can be host. Not going into any more details right now, if you want to know send me a note with 'pound me' in the subject line.

Looking For A Loaded Bladder - m4w - 30

Any ladies out there into giving golden showers and more? Looking to be a human toilet. Email me, let's talk. Married, if you can host that would be great, saves on hotel costs.

Two Brothers - m4w - 26

Hi we are two brothers married and bored looking to have some fun tonight! We are willing to do anything. Send a pic get a pic and we do not care about looks or anything like that. Any size welcome to apply. Get back to me.

Married Hot Looking Sexy Guy -Curious –

Over 6 foot tall - 190 lbs - very sexy and smooth - I want to orally please another man. MUST BE EXTREMELY clean - married prefer also. First time inquiry.

Need Discreet Massage - m4w - 47

I am looking for a discreet woman that is available for a regular massage and more? I can help with gas money. I am usually available during the day. Self employed can skip out. I am always very clean and respectable. I am married so we need to be discreet. Big plus if you can host. I prefer thin, age is open (over 18). Please be clean and open to an adult relationship. If there is a connection, willing to do this often. I am not interested in head games. Not willing to pay for services rendered. Trade only.

Removing My Ring - m4w - 41

Hot ladies that are not able to be satisfied please read on. 45 yr old average married man that likes to wild sex. 6'2' 210, financially secure, willing to buy you a cell phone and pay bill. If you have an available morning or afternoon free this week, please indicate so, if you have a photo that would be nice. Think nice mutual location, lunch or maybe dinner, drinks and romantic candle light. It only gets better from there. You must be able to keep a secret.

Remember When? - m4w - 31

Married man missing how it used to be with my wife.
I miss the passion and desire, the unknown, the nervous touching and playing. I want to kiss, hold and taste for the first time all over again. I am not looking for a serious relationship. Sex only, I do have a wife.

Married Man Seeks Partner for Wild Times - m4w - 26

I am an attractive, fit and sexy guy who has been neglected due to conflicting work schedules and interests. Also, my partner is very close minded and self conscious when it comes to sex. I'm more of a kinky, experimental person who enjoys things like oral, anal, role playing, fetishes, etc. My goal is to find somebody similar to myself who is looking for someone to be kinky and a little nasty with. Needs to be DD free and willing to be tied up and whipped.

This profile is for SERIOUS girls only, no men, no pros.

Str8 Married With Damn To Be Released!

Wondering if anyone is out there. You cum by here pick me up and then I blow a huge load in your mouth! I am muscular, handsome, large dick and straight. MUST BE DISCREET my family is important to me. I do not have a car.

Breast Worshipper Here! - m4w - 31

Do you enjoy having your breasts fondled, squeezed, licked, sucked, nibbled on, rubbed, and basically worshipped? Want to squeeze your tittys around a large throbbing masterpiece? Would you like to? wm, 5'10", 185 lb. Just shy of 7 inches. Daytimes during the week (yes, I am married) discretion a must and guaranteed. I am a lawyer and have a contract.

"The New Awareness of Relationships"

JOURNAL

Dear Diary,

You are my fond companion who holds all of my secrets. You never doubt me or question me. You only listen. Never being judgmental or condescending, you are a true friend. A companion and my priest for confession.

You have helped me through inconceivable periods in my life. If my written words could cry, the ink would have run to form its own river. You have all the pieces of me. Desires, hopes, dreams and little secrets.

On this day, I proudly announce the end of my mourning. The footprints stamped in my heart have since been removed. The crack has been repaired, I am a new person.

I have healed. I am whole, I am well, and I am woman!

Internet dating only proved to me there are Ted's everywhere. I wasn't and am not alone. I could not believe how many profiles are of married men. I was very shocked at how honest those married men were. Husbands who are so willing to throw their marriages away for the sake of getting laid or their ego shined. Dirty events they keep from their partners. I did review some profiles of single guys but I was so scarred by the married profiles, my internet dating experiment was over.

It has occurred to me that I can make a difference in the lives of strangers. When these wives discover the truth about their other halves, it will hurt but, in the long run, it is for the best. Either marriages will be fixed or destroyed. Either way the truth is revealed. I personally never had it within me to forgive but I'm sure there are women stronger than me.

You may find this crazy but I decided to dust off those stilettos sitting in that box, buried deep in my closet. I dressed to the nines tonight and plan on heading back out into the real world, to breathe life and lust deep in my lungs and soul.

After dressing beyond sexy and glancing in the mirror, I felt vindicated. That jackass ex-husband of mine was a fool with his deception. He really screwed things up for his race, for I am now "The Other Woman".

As I slipped my graceful manicured tootsies into my sexy pumps, I felt like a superhero putting on a cape. The Other Woman is here to save the day, one wife at a time!

Chloe

Dear Chloe,

I met your husband last night.....

I walked into a dimly lit lounge of a local upscale restaurant. The atmosphere screamed wealth and the wait staff looked airbrushed. Bottles of wine were suspended from the ceiling each with their own story to evolve when uncorked.

Lights bounced off of magical martini glasses, soft laughter and conversation filled the air mixed in with a beautiful harmony of classical music. You could get drunk just on the environment.

I scanned the crowd at the long lavish bar, deciding where I should be seated. Sure, I could have sat down in any of the empty bar stools but the one next to your husband looked more inviting.

To put your mind at ease, I had no idea who this gorgeous man was or even if he was taken, I was merely looking for companionship for the evening. Do I get paid for sex? Heavens no, I am not that kind of girl. I have sex for free!

I took my position at the bar and he glanced over to see who had entered his arena. A quick look of astonishment widened into a smile and then the ultimate internal thinking of, "Wow...who are you?" moved through his brain and left his lips as, "Hi!"

The bartender approached us and placed a coaster down on the bar in front of me. He was a very handsome distinguished man with a black bow tie. His teeth seemed too perfect to be his own and when he smiled, an adorable dimple appeared on his chin. He asked me if I wanted to see a cocktail or wine menu. I asked for both and he handed them to me and strolled away for a moment.

As I was studying the array of elaborate alcohol concoctions, I could feel your husband's eyes studying the full length of me. To help him with his imagination, I uncrossed and then re-crossed my legs. The black snug silk dress I was wearing had a very high slit up my tanned leg; I was giving him quite the show. I wondered what he thought about the garter. It was, after all, an icon of sexiness.

The adorable bartender returned and I ordered a girly cocktail. Your husband requested that the bartender put it on his tab. I was flattered...okay, not really, because it happens more times than not. Truth be told, it was one of the reasons why I sat down next to him. Women can tell easily which men are easy targets for a night on the town for free. Being polite, I had turned to face him, flipped my long chocolate hair back, licked my luscious pink lips and softly thanked him, all the while batting my long eyelashes and maintaining eye contact. He was suckered at that moment.

Your husband, just like the hundreds (maybe thousands?) before him, began the next sentence with, "So....." Past that, it doesn't waver much, but he continued with, "...Are you waiting for someone?"

Giving him another good look over, "charming" was my first thought. Not that I normally pay attention to aura, but he did seem to have a radiant glow about him. He had some kind of magnetism which just pulled you in. I am sure his distinctive impression was left with many long after he was gone.

I stole a peek to see if there was a wedding ring, and you would have been proud, he was wearing it. I have seen a lot of tanned lines on ring fingers and way too many magic ring-disappearing acts to count. The engraved gold on his finger shimmered with diamonds; your taste in jewelry is noted.

I answered his question with "No, actually I just finished a dinner meeting and thought I would come in here before leaving".

Your handsome man replied "Lucky me!"

God had blessed me with a great imagination. Visual images began floating through my head of straddling him on his bar stool. To gain control over the ride I was picturing, I placed the spiked heels of my leather stilettos against the hard brass part of the stool and was off to the rodeo.

Are you wondering who I am?

Allow me to tell you about me. I am the woman your mother warned him about. I exude sex appeal. Regardless of the man's preference---blonde, brunette or redhead---I capture their attention. I am a world class beauty, in a gown or a baseball cap. I am funny, smart and, most importantly, I know how to listen to a man, to make them feel special and important. I radiate confidence. When I meet a man, he walks away thinking that, on that day, his life has changed. Men respond to me, and even women respond to me. My eyes are gold in color, and I have long dark hair which I love to play with. Olive skin covers an hourglass figure. I have had no elective surgeries; God made me this way. I have a sexy smile with a sensual, husky bedroom voice. And, unlike the 99% of internet profiles people write, every word of this is true.

Back to your husband and away from my erotic vision.

I smiled back, "Lucky you, huh?"

He leaned in close enough to inhale my perfume. "I wish I could be the chair you are sitting on, even for just a moment." Creative thought was stamped across his forehead. When I was a teenager, it was my bicycle seat the boys wanted to be. They don't change much as they grow up.

He was so close to me, I was inhaling the alcohol on his breath. His sense of smell was also working. "Your perfume smells really good. "He reached for my hand and wrapped his own around it. His skin was warm. I could have sworn I glimpsed a spark of electricity from the contact.

The bartender snapped a stare at me as if to ask if I was okay. I nodded a quick, appreciative smile, and turned my attention back to your husband.

"Do you think I am a good-looking man?" He was lightly tracing my palm in the pattern of a heart.

My eyes scanned the length of him. Easing back into my seat, fiddling with the fruity umbrella in my glass, I told him the truth. "I do."

The evening progressed with more cocktails for me, and at some stage, he switched to water. He relayed the fight the two of you had earlier in the day during which you accused him of cheating. He was hurt and very tired of defending himself. He had a rich fantasy life but never acted upon it. I believed him.

As your husband continued pouring his soul out to me, I couldn't help but sense he is one of those guys that will get better-looking with age. Interesting how that works. He may have been a dog in his youth but look at him now. Women are usually not that fortunate.

I queried on how you two met. He loved telling me that story. His eyes grew bright; the memory was obviously a fond one. He also spoke about your three kids, all in high school at the same time. My curiosity took an additional turn upwards, so I probed deeper.

I was absorbed in this repartee of ours. Resting my chin on my hand, I inquired "Why does she accuse you of cheating?"

Given the circumstance, it was kind of an ironic question. He told me of all the traveling he does for work, and of your long work hours, chauffeuring the kids to all their sports and after-school events. He is bored. Your sex life has been the same for too many years. You never surprise him anymore by dropping to your knees while he is brushing his teeth. *Hummer* is only a vehicle sitting in the driveway. Sexy lingerie lies in your dresser, most with the tags still attached. He spoke of all the hot voicemails you used to leave him, distant memories now. Phone sex? Not in years. His facial expression grew despairing as our conversation went further.

Excusing himself to the restroom, I pondered what I would think of my husband sitting on a barstool and rambling on and on to some stranger about the intimate details of my life. Some guys believe that by discussing their bad relationships, women may feel sorry for them and they could have a better chance of getting laid. If men understood really understood us, they would realize the majority of females screw for love, not lust or sympathy. Priding myself as being an exception, I roll around in the sack because I am a savior super hero and well, I love experiencing the big "O".

When he returned, your man lightly placed his hand on my back as he sat down. Step one, buy drinks. Step two, touch me. His hands were still thermal. My dress had an open back, so his skin was touching mine. My visions came back to me. A golden rule I will share with you is this…"Always bring a change of panties". Our bodies react like men when stimulated, except we can make more of a mess. I picture you nodding.

Our conversations seemed to be all over the map; our work, travels, kids, and most interesting to him, my very own love life. I really liked him. He was witty and very provocative without even trying. He was a strong man by the looks of it, if cradled in his arms, one could only feel safe.

Last call, my bartender/protector called out. We both decline. He explained to me that he was not planning on going home that night. Is your marriage over? Maybe. Was there truth in his ramblings? Maybe he *had* become your very own punching bag. Only you know the answer to that question. Have you finally destroyed your marriage?

I sat there wondering what to do next. My hormones were pushing me to take him to the nearest hotel and bang his lights out. Do I find out if he is as terrific in bed as I think, or do I help you out? You are more of a stranger than he is. Was this gentleman ready to be a cheater, an adulterer?

He whispered, "Come with me."

I whispered back while cradling my face in the nook of his neck, "I could easily cum with you, but maybe you need to take some more time before throwing in the towel."

He laughed and thanked me for the compliment. It was then time to leave.

He was a gentleman, settling up the tab; then helping me with my jacket. He stood behind me, slid the fur over my delicate shoulders and kissed my shoulder. His breath was steaming and I felt myself melting further. If I could have been a fruit at that moment, I would have been a melon, for I was producing dew.

Your husband walked me to my car door, gently grabbed my waist, turning my face upwards to meet his and planted a kiss on me I felt throughout my entire body. He really knew how to kiss. It takes a lot to buckle my knees but your husband succeeded. Passion and desire raged through both of us.

He opened my car; I slipped into the driver's seat and happen to glance at the stick shift. Opps, my car is an automatic. Silently cursing my lack of good manners, all I wanted to do was grab it and put it into gear. He closed the car door. Oh, well.

Still standing in the same spot as I drove away, he waved goodbye, I blew a kiss and headed down the roadway. You will be fuming to know he kissed me, but it was a lot less than what could have been. You won't produce a "thank you" for me, but you should be grateful for the fact I walked away. We both walked away. I did my part, and the rest is up to you. Change your relationship, starting today. Reignite the spark, shut-up and listen more. Why, because, next time I may not be so kind. My mission is to enlighten wives about cheating husbands, not to make one an adulterer.

He tracked me down several weeks later. I had told him that night where I worked. I agreed to meet him for lunch. Leaving the office, I was wondering to myself why I did that. This get together was breaking one of my golden rules - Never, ever see the husbands again. Yours was special though. I was so thrilled to have met someone who never cheated on his wife that I was willing to trash my code of conduct for him.

We had lunch, and he stammered a little bit, and began with, "I am not sure if you are from heaven or hell, whether you are a vixen or an angel. I am not sure if your assignment on earth is to break up marriages or help preserve them."

I am genuinely dumbfounded by this bizarre statement.

"I went home that night, woke up my wife from her sleep and told her all about you."

Speechless on my behalf is an understatement. I had scanned the restaurant, looking for you and your weapon of choice to cause bodily damage. I was having thoughts of diving under the table if I did see you but then my senses kicked in and told me I would forget you were there and I would find myself eating lunch from your husband's lap.

He continued "We talked a lot, and cried, and when we we're tired of talking, we made love and had wild sex." He had such an energized look on his face as he spoke. Your husband was very happy.

I was still thinking about Polish sausage for lunch. He is Polish, right?

I Met Your Husband Last Night

He reached across the table, snatched my hand and softly stroked it. "I asked you to meet me today so I could thank you."

When I left our lunch saying goodbye for the last time, I decided I envy you. You have a man who really loves you. You hit the lottery lady, a one in a million chance! Don't screw it up!

Best of Wishes,
The Other Woman

"FAITH"

JOURNAL

Dear Diary,

I could not help but continue throughout the evening to think of tonight's married man. My lingering desire for him will soon pass. But it's not that, I have some issues with his wife.

This couple had been married for a very long time, during which time he remained faithful.

I had seen firsthand what his frustration looked like. He tried to be a good boy, he appreciated beauty but he genuinely loved his wife. Her husband never stuck his poker anywhere else but in her fire. However his wife was making it hot as hell in there, closely causing him to jump from the flames.

Rarely do I run across a man like him. Sure, I could have pushed the envelope but, for a moment and only a moment, I pictured his wife. This lucky woman who was screwing up the marriage by not trusting. I understand it is very difficult to trust. Look at me. However, if a wife had never been given a reason to doubt, she has no excuse.

What is the point in having a relationship without trust? In college or grade school, everyone starts the marking period with an "A". Then it's up to the student to keep it. I view relationships the same way. We start out with trust, and then we need to work on keeping it. However, once it's broken, I feel there is no possible way to repair it. Those who say they have forgiven their partner are lying through their teeth or are really Christian to their souls. Forgive those who trespass against us. Sorry sweet Jesus, maybe you had forgotten to make me with that trait. Cheated once again.

Did this husband actually do something to break it? In this case, I think not. My belief is the wife was scorned by someone else in her previous life or maybe because she is aging she feels less desired by her husband. She could have easily ruined the relationship. He came forward with the truth (which took balls). She needs to be thankful for it and be grateful for being one of the lucky ones.

It takes two to screw up a relationship and it takes one to walk away.

Do men ultimately commit the crime they are accused of? Some. Why? If their life is going to be miserable for doing something they are not doing, they might as well do it. Really, I have been told this.

TRUST
To Remember Unity Stays Together

The reference he made at lunch about the vixen and angel was off the wall. As he was speaking, my mind flipped into pictures, I am a visual thinker. I could see an angel and a devil sitting on each of his shoulders, just like in the cartoons. Except my vision was not rated "G". The angel was wearing a chastity belt and the devil had his throbbing tail in his hands.

I am off work tomorrow. It's been a while since I have visited the family; I need to swing by the family gathering spot and say "hello".

Paige

Dear Paige,

I met your husband last night.....

Let me first start by informing you that you must not be very bright. There are unintelligent people everywhere; maybe you are smart but certainly lacking in common sense and in the women's intuition department.

Your husband is a dirt bag and, from what I gathered from him, you have no idea. Time to smarten up Chickie! I'm going to show you the way.

I feel it's my job to tell you what you may not want to know. Don't ask why, for the reason is not important to you. But I will say this; I woke one morning to find myself single. I began to analyze my life. Would I really want a husband again?

Every day when I have chance encounters with another woman's husband, it enables me to examine my single situation further. Sometimes a wart growth of a guy enters my life briefly that pretty much guarantees that I want to be single for a long, long time. A wart like your husband.

My family owns a chain of strip clubs. Yes, seedy places where women dance naked on stages and men are tucking dollar bills in their g-strings. I don't work there, nor have I ever. But if I want to see certain family members of mine, that is where I must go. Some of the family, in essence, lives there. Everyone must make a living and this is where my family makes theirs. Sex is a powerful enterprise.

These establishments, regardless of what city in the country they are located, resemble Las Vegas. Everything is shiny and more times than not, very tacky. Welcome to the adult sexual fantasy playgrounds. Where mirrors and lighting make everyone look good and individuals reach into the perverted parts of their souls and fulfill desires which they keep as secrets.

In case you have never visited such an enterprise, let me fill you in a little. When you pull into the drive, service is everything. Your husband and all the other clients are treated like gold. Even the valet parking makes them feel like a king. The car parkers are usually dressed in suits or some kind of uniform. The lots are built with fences. This helps the covert operation, using it as a cover for prying eyes. You can sometimes see a bopping head through the window of a parked car.

When you walk in, they offer a coat check. A really sexy girl is there to greet them and handle their belongings. The clubs are air conditioned, so the firm thing's teats could cut glass. Nobody ever really looks at her face. It's the first place money changes hands. Some clubs charge a cover; some do not. Many have required dress codes for their patrons.

White collar workers tend to go to the bars that serve steak and lobster, while the blue collar workers prefer to spend their money strictly on dancers and alcohol. Yes, there is such a thing as low class and high class titty bars. Some clubs even circumvent the laws by running a juice bar so the dancers are completely naked.

Once in the building, the customers are escorted, based on who they are and how much they spend, to a seating section. Your husband has a front-row view. He's a big shot. His platinum status earns him his own couch while he is there.

There is one large stage in the center of the bar and smaller stages scattered throughout the balance of the floor. The poles extend from the stage, floor to ceiling. Mirrors encompass the walls. A DJ booth will be located in one of the corners. Large bouncers walk around to keep order. The bartenders are usually those women who can't dance anymore because gravity has kicked in.

Although you would imagine it is uncommon for women who are not dancing to be in such a place, you would be sadly mistaken, as many couples do come here. An erotic adventure! Scores of women have fantasies of other females; the lesbian side of them comes out. Other times they are just curious. Girls will also get lap dances, while their date watches. Their date can be their very own husband. To each their own.

Your husband had roaming eyes and approached me. He was a balding guy with a comb over, a wrinkled suit and the bottom of his shirt hanging over his belt. "Hey!" he said with a slight southern accent.

As if that is any kind of introduction.

He is speaking and attempting to tuck his shirt in at the same time. "My name is Sam".

Like I really care.

He proceeded to enlighten me that he is wealthy and was packing some major explosives in his pants. Gross is the only word to describe what I was thinking.

I noticed the tan line and couldn't help myself from inquiring about you. He informed me that you were at home. I had asked him if you knew he was there.

Your husband was a little temperamental; annoyed, he responded "No".

He was inclined, though, to tell me you are aware he came to places like that club for business.

"Really?" was the answer I had given him, almost choking on my laugh.

I thought to myself "Wifey needs to get a clue! ".

He began blabbing that you believe there was no touching involved. Apparently, state law prohibits it and you bought that load of crap. Not that there are not state laws, there are in most states. The bullshit part is the fine for a patron touching a dancer can be as little as ten dollars. Do you think your husband can afford that? Not that the police raid these places, some are customers just like your husband. Many are bought off with favors from the bar.

The DJ will announce a dancer and she will come onto the stage, oiled down and cosmetically altered, reeking of raw sex. She generally will start with some clothing on and, as the music continues to play, she will initiate stripping. It really is an erotic showing. The dancers are flexible and the pole allows them to demonstrate just how far a woman really can bend over. The men watch as she touches herself and imitates sexual gratification. Personally I think their nerve endings are no longer functioning, they must be worn out from excessive stimulation.

Those men not fortunate enough to be seated by a stage will walk to the edge of it and place a folded bill between their teeth. Motioning for the dancer to come over and spread her legs. The stripper glides over in her five-inch heels and squats before them, while using her hand to slide over the tooth-floss g-string. The guy leans over the stage and puts his head between her legs. He inserts money. Yes, it is a sexual act! On television, the men insert the bills with their hands under garters on the dancer's legs. Reality is much different!

I had to assume you have no idea how often your husband visited that bar. Surprise! He is there EVERY DAY! Yep, you thought he was at work and, instead, your husband has been sitting in that club. His office staff is trained in telling you when you call he was in with a client or on another call. His "sexitary" in lightening speed, sends him a text message letting him know you had phoned.

How many times did you get this phone call back from your husband? "Hi Honey, sorry I'm in a meeting, it's still going to be a couple hours, I snuck out for a minute to let you know I was thinking about you. Gotta run and get back in there." Sound familiar? And you thought it was lovable that he called you.

He knows everyone by name, the waitress always remembers his drink order and he is such a good client, the club considered him VIP status. He was spending anywhere from $500-$1000 a day there. Although your household income could afford it, he had you cutting coupons to save money. See a problem here?

The club does cash advances but, just in case anyone's wife looks at the credit card statements, it shows a clever marketing company name, not the strip club's name. Yes, it's a conspiracy.

While the dancer on center stage twirls, bends and stoops; other strippers are circulating the club's floor offering lap dances. The fee for this primal humping can range from twenty to fifty dollars. The men apply a firm hold to the girl's hips for added pressured pleasure.

Your husband loves lap dances and suckling on the boobies of these ladies while they are riding him hard. Alcohol somehow enables these men to forget there was someone right before them who did the same exact thing. If a dancer was ever killed right after work, I pity the forensic teams extracting the different DNA from her breasts.

There is a section in the back of the bar for the VIP's and when your husband is really getting it on, he escapes behind the security guarded curtain. Wonder what he is doing in there? Please use your imagination at this point.

I had seen him on other visits I have had to the club but last night was the first time I talked with him. Because my clothes were on, often it is sexier than the naked women bending over. He offered me $500 to strip for him. While he asked for the impossible, his hand was rubbing my butt. This is a family business and customers like him pay their bills, so I actually had to tolerate your husband.

I glanced over and under one of the high-tops (a standing up table), I noticed a man with his penis in his hand. He was stroking away to the beat of the music. Excusing myself from your husband to notify security, the gentleman was immediately escorted from the club. This happens often; I guess they just can't help themselves.

Leaving the immediate area, I headed to the restroom. Want to see something wild? That's the place to go. The women's restroom is also used as the area where the dancers change from outfit to outfit. Twenty to thirty naked women are overcrowded in this area, each with a chip on their shoulder for one reason or another. Two of them were arguing over your husband. Mr. Big Shot split the money he normally spent on one dancer between both. Neither one was happy about the situation. They each wanted it all. Making matters even more hectic, the costume lady showed up. She makes handmade fantasy clothing and sells them in the bathroom to the dancers. The boob bouncing chickies pushed each other to get to the rack. The better the guise, the more money they might make. I washed my hands and left the chaos behind. Your husband then followed me from the ladies room to a far part of the building and started up again.

Curiosity just killing me, I inquired more about his life. You two have only been married for a couple of years. Right now, you are pregnant. He does not consider pregnancy beautiful, he finds it repulsive. This means he finds you repulsive. He told me that before the two of you were married, you actually caught him with another woman. You turned a blind eye to it.

Stupid, Stupid Woman. I am not expecting you to believe me but I am requesting you review the credit card bills. It's not a marketing company which appears on his statement and the perfumed odor following him in the door is not his office's air freshener.

I heard from one of the dancers last night that your man has another baby on the way. I am cheerful to hear he is successful, because Lord knows you deserve alimony! The dancer believes he loves her and she recognizes a great meal ticket.

One day he came home to you and there were bugs flying around his crotch area. Remember that day? He blamed it on the orange juice he spilled at breakfast and told you it was fruit flies. Uh, uh...it was crabs. Please schedule a doctor's visit for yourself as soon as possible.

Just so you know, at the end of the night when the lights get turned on and the club needs to be cleaned, you can find used condoms scattered throughout the floor.

Those lap dances are pretty hot; men will go into the restroom and put a condom on their pal. They will order another lap dance and explode like a shaken up soda. I guess some of these low lifes are just too lazy to return to the restroom, so they unzip and toss it to the floor.

One night for shits and giggles, I polled one of the bars. Over 80% of the men in attendance happened to be married. I would hope that speaks volumes to you, as you can see that by the high percentage, you are not even close to being alone.

Another thing which really astonishes me is the fact these entire establishments are filled with horny men, each getting off next to each other. And they think that is not gay? The homophobes are the ones which I have issues with. If they are revolted by gay men, how can they get an erection with all of these other guys? Obviously having two hundred men being turned on at the same time must be erotic to them. Of course, I could never find a man to admit it. Did you call the attorney yet?

I Feel Dirty Just Writing This,
The Other Woman

"Dancing Out of the Marriage"

JOURNAL

Dear Diary,

Any wife who does not have a problem with their husband going to a strip club on a regular basis is out of her flipping mind!

I personally know a few wives like that. They think "Aw, what's the harm, my husband is only looking." There is damage! I am not talking about the guys who go in a group because someone is getting married or even those who entertain for out of town clients. I am speaking of those dudes stopping weekly or, in many cases, daily.

Always by themselves.

Porno is something these men cannot touch. Live naked beings in front of them for sale, they can. Sometimes the dancers are so giving; they may even share a disease or two. Very sweet of them, don't you think?

Not all of the dancers have their own prostitution ring phenomenon but many can be bought cheaply. The minority are college students, the majority are not. It's a job to them, nothing personal. They need to feed their kids and someone else's husband is the ideal one to do it. You can't hold culpable the dancers for making a living; its husbands like Paige who fuel that part of the economy.

Some of those clubs do have hot dancers, but many do not. Technology has developed a lighting system to disguise what they really look like. Dancers do have stretch marks and cellulite; the patrons just can't see it. Everyone looks good on stage. Alcohol also helps alter one's vision.

The balance of the bar is extremely dark, their flaws cannot be seen then either. So basically the husbands wives' *are* dancing for them, their just too stupid to recognize it.

Drugs may flow by like water under a bridge. It's just a giant daily/nightly party. Ask who is hosting your husband's next golf outing.

Then there are the women who have no idea, such as Paige. Their husbands are the lowest scum of all. I hope their penises rot off.

I have always told my married friends about strip clubs and, for those who would not believe me; I just took them for a personal tour. Afterward I would hand them my attorney's card.

PS: Today is my one-year anniversary in my new home.

Good Night!

Rachel

Dear Rachel,

I met your husband last night.....

Waking in the morning, I strolled into my bathroom, dropped my robe and turned on the shower. There is nothing better than a hot shower massaging your body.

When I was looking at purchasing a new home, one item of luxury that the house just had to have was strong water pressure. The contractor who built my home added an additional upgrade, free of charge mind you, of the most unbelievable shower head. That story is about Carol's husband, not yours, so I won't bother going into further detail about him now. This narrative is only about your handsome husband.

I adjusted the shower head to angle towards the built-in sitting bench. I sat my firm tush down and leaned slightly back, placing my hands against the glass wall. That always sparks the thought of being tied up.

I closed my eyes. The pulsing action of the water was amazing. I felt as if I was being devoured in the hottest of love sessions.

Don't act so surprised. I know that in the privacy of bathrooms, we girls attempt this all the time. I'm sure you have one of those showerheads which unclip and it has a hose extending out from it. This is so we can maneuver it anywhere we want it to go. Marketed as an item to wash the shampoo from our hair, we girls are smart; we knew what to really do with it. Yes, you would be correct in thinking it was invented by a woman. Isn't it funny how women never discuss this sexual endeavor with their friends?

I am a visual thinker, and my fantasies play in my head with moving images like an X-rated flick. The material is always fresh and near, with powerful images of men, like your husband.

It was another man that morning which filled my vision, and I could feel myself beginning to swell.

I changed my position and changed the angle on the shower head to match. Bending over, I placed my hands on the bench. As I moved, the spray of the water pounded my mammillas, which brought only deeper pleasure.

The images in my mind soared with the physical sensations, and the moans of ecstasy soon followed. Turning off the shower, my day was off to a perfect start!

I stood before my dressing mirror and dried off. I had noticed the evidence of a previous night's play. Debra's husband had a little too much fun and a few too many hungers.

There were still bite marks and hickies in the pattern of an arrow starting between my breasts and leading all the way down to my pelvic bone. I am normally not a fan of being temporarily tattooed, but I could not help but still find humor in my situation.

I had put on an adorable button-up dress and grabbed my keys to head out the door. One last glance in the mirror had confirmed I was looking hot!

Opening the door and walking down the path, my neighbor waved hello right away and smiled a big lusty grin. I love to tease that guy. My two-seater already had the top down; I clicked the button on the key ring which opened the small trunk.

Normally, I would have just tossed my handbag in there and go, but the moment called for a show. The dress was short and on the tight side, I bent over low to match the height of the car and put my bag in.

My panties were in the bag instead of on me because I was still wet from my shower play. I figured I would put them on later after the sun warmed and dried me a little. The sun always laps up moisture.

I could feel the dress cupping the lower part of my buns, which meant he was seeing quite a lot of me. I'm sure my kitty was in full view.

I had heard a scream, wheeled around, and realize he had been startled by his wife coming out of their home. He spun around with the water hose in his hand, and soaked her.

Two wet women for him to think about!

I jumped in the car and gave them a friendly wave as I drove off. I was late for a meeting, so I pressed the pedal and zipped out of the neighborhood.

It was a picture-perfect day, and I felt as if I could conquer the world.

Are you wondering at this time why I have given you all of this other information about my day? I sense it's important for you to understand the type of girl your husband had fallen prey to.

Cruising at a comfortable speed, I adjusted my *Ray-Bans* and swiped away a strand of hair which was tickling my face. The car beside me on the road had a really cute driver, smiling, holding his cell as he mouthed a request for my number. Boys will be boys.

I accelerated and he was doing a great job keeping speed with me. I blew him a kiss, and sized him up right away as a single man. I have no desire for single men. I am not seeking a relationship. I prefer married men; I need to stay focused to my mission.

In his haste of playing with me, he slammed right into the car which had slowed down in front of him. The car he hit jumped into my lane, and I collided with the same vehicle.

My tiny car did surprisingly well, considering the speed I was traveling at, and everyone appeared okay. I was stuck in my car however, my seatbelt would not unbuckle.

Someone had called the police, and they arrived quickly. A fire/rescue truck pulled up, too.

The police officer motioned a fireman to my car. Yes, your adorable husband. They both stood outside my door, and from the looks of it, they were very happy to see me. My dress had climbed very high, and I was in plain view. If I was a cartoon, part of me would be meowing.

There was nothing in the car to cover me. Even if there was, I'm certain I would not have used it. Their expressions were too much fun. That whole "make sure you have clean underwear on in case you are in accident" advice rumbled through my head. My clean underwear was still in a bag located in the trunk.

The guys paused grinning long enough to figure out how to get me out of my car. The fireman walked to his truck and returned with shears and very quickly cut me out of there.

He lifted me out and onto a gurney, and I protested, "Really, Mr. Handsome Fireman, I am fine, and all this is unnecessary."

"Miss, I am a professional, and this was a serious accident, so I must be adamant that I check you out."

He wheeled me to a just-arrived ambulance, covering me with a sheet in the process. I was disappointed; I enjoyed the idea they were looking at me. Oh well, another time perhaps. He and another fireman slid me into the back of the vehicle.

The other fireman shut the door and walked towards the front of the ambulance; I could hear the engine start. Your husband had begun to check my vitals.

"Miss, I need to unbutton your dress so I can listen to your heart" he said seriously.

"Please, I wouldn't want something to be wrong with my heart, I am such a giving person, my heart is very important." I said while batting my long eyelashes at him. Pathetic, I know, but these yo-yo's fall for the helplessness of a girl all the time.

His fingers touched the first button on my dress. I couldn't help but think, "Wow, this was hot". I could feel my breasts just dying to be sprung from their cage. I was not wearing a bra, I never do. My breasts are perfect, so why wear one?

He had about four buttons undone. "Miss, your dress is very tight; I would have a difficult time putting the stethoscope where it needs to be placed. There are only a few remaining buttons. With your permission, I would like to just undo them all".

I realized I wouldn't be wearing my panties for awhile because I was getting wet again. "Please, whatever you need to do". When he was finished with the rest of the buttons, he peeled back my dress, opening side to side.

The stethoscope was cold but his hands were very warm. I was completely exposed to him. A fleeting thought crossed my mind. I wondered if he could tell my kitten was drooling.

He had to bend really close to my chest to listen to my heart. He asked me to breathe in and exhale. My chest rose in the air. I may have helped it a little more by arching my back and then without warning, one of my hard chocolate kisses brushed against his lips.

I thought the vehicle was moving but I could not be sure. All I can do was reflect about this husband of yours. What was he going to do about this situation?

He asked me to breathe in and out again. Obliging, the same thing happened. I looked to his crouch and could see his snake was releasing its venom. He had a wet spot. "One more time, Miss." the result was the same. That time he opened his mouth and sucked on it like the piece of candy it was!

I knew that day was going to be a good day. He had taken the straps on the gurney and tied my hands above me. Yippee, reliving part of that shower I had earlier. He went to the foot of the bed and tied my ankles down but not before lifting the gynecological stirrups where he had placed my feet.

He unzipped his pants, climbed on top of me and inserted his king cobra. Though the gurney was locked into position, there was still enough give, that with the motion of us, it did slightly slide back and forth.

It did not take long for both of us to thank God! Good thing too, because his partner in the front seat announced we just arrived at the hospital.

I asked him only one question. "What made you cheat on your wife with me today?

As he was getting himself dressed, he turned to me with a sly expression.

"My wife, who is never happy with me, said I can never follow even the simplest of instructions. I made an assurance to her that I would pay more attention to details and try harder."

I wondered why you, his wife, would give him *those* kind of instructions.

He continued. "She informs me she should not have to ask me to do things, I should just do them."

Ok, I had no idea where he was taking his story line.

He continued "An example would be putting dishes in the dishwasher. If the dirty dishes are right there in front of me, it's a sign they need to be put in the washer. I shouldn't have to be asked, I ought to just pay attention and do it."

I was still lost.

"When I unbuttoned your dress, I was just following instructions. The arrow on your chest was a sign telling me what to do!"

Satisfied with living up to your expectations, he kissed me goodbye.

He finally learned to listen to you and follow the signs laid out before him.

Placing the sheet back over me, he wheeled me to the attendant at the hospital who was waiting for us.

Great Job Training Him but Dump Him!
The Other Woman

Sara

Dear Sara,

I met your husband last night.....

Let me tell you, I was having a heck of a day. I was caught up in a car accident, I had the most stimulating ambulance ride and then finished up at the hospital.

The collision was minor and I don't believe there was anything wrong with me. Medical professionals are always doing things out of precaution and possible litigation.

I had a meeting I could not attend, my car had been towed to Lord only knows where and then I was stuck at the hospital for at least a couple of hours.

I was so happy to have met your husband. His company helped the time pass quickly.

When I arrived, I was put into a room. God those places smell bad, I could hear people crying and I was lucky enough to be in the next room from someone violently vomiting. I then had begun to feel woozy myself.

There was only some kind of sheet suspended from the ceiling to separate the makeshift rooms. Those curtains never close all the way. It's like being at the zoo because every person who walks by feels the need to peek in your opening.

Your husband walked in the unit I was occupying, just like he did a thousand times in the past. His eyes were down upon his entry studying my chart. "Car accident, huh?", then he glanced up away from his chart and looked me.

"Oh, I'm sorry; I must have the wrong bed!" He had this quizzical look on his face.

I replied "Do you have another car accident patient right now?"

He scratched the side of his head "Well, no but..."

I followed the direction of his eyes to my legs.

Laughing nervously "Oh, the stir-ups."

Looking back at my face he said "Your chart is not listing injuries which would require you to be in those stir-ups."

My expression resembled a cat that just chewed up a mouse.

"Actually Doctor, I believe the only injuries I have are the strap marks on my wrists and ankles."

With a coy smirk, he made the following offer. "If I untie you and put the bed back to its normal condition, will you tell me how you ended up like this? You appear to be in good spirits, I take it you were not forced."

I agreed.

Let me tell you my impression of your husband. He is older than me but in great shape. I could see his muscle tone through his jacket. He knew he was good looking, which is why he wore his lab jacket snug.

He had dark hair with gorgeous strands of grey running through it. Not that coarse wiry hair but soft white in color. He is of Italian decent with perfect teeth and a charming smile. He stood about 6'2" and was graced with being proportionate in height and weight. He had deep blue eyes, long dark eye lashes and was extremely sexy.

He was the perfect specimen of a male. I had quickly formed the opinion that you are a fortunate woman. I would smile waking each day next to him!

I considered for a moment what it would be like to be married to a doctor. He loves his career. Do you get to act out his profession in the bedroom? Is there a box of latex gloves and gel in the bedside drawer? Does he ask you to stick your tongue out and he places something in there? How about drugs, does he slip you anything to help you relax?

I began to tell him my story, starting from that morning. Hey, why not? I had an audience, might as well share. Spreading the love, that's all!

He enjoyed my shower scene. He actually had started to develop a sweat on his forehead. I had to include in all of the little details and asked if he was a visual thinker, he said "No". That left me with no alternative but to act out the parts physically for him. Let me inform you, your husband sure had a great bedside manner; he listened very intently to every word I said.

He inquired where I lived but that's one thing I never tell, if I don't have to. My home is like a bat cave, the less men who know about it, the better.

I moved onto the story of the accident, then the fireman and of course your husband was surprised when he seen the hicky arrow on my torso. His question was answered. I finished by telling him "That's how I ended up strapped to the gurney."

He laughed again and adjusted his pants. Of course he was aroused, I mean, how could he not be? It was a pretty hot story!

Raising an eyebrow, I inquired "Do you need some help down there Doctor?"

His eyes smiled that time and he said "I guess I have run out of room!"

I used my hand and stroked him gently at first, proceeding by grabbing him through his clothes and holding on tight! "I would love to help you find more room."

A nurse walked in. Gosh, I almost had forgotten I was in the hospital!

"Doctor, I need you to sign this discharge." The nurse spoke with such distaste in her voice. She had the aura of a bitchy broad.

I was sitting in bed with the sheet tucked under my arms, it was apparent I was not wearing a hospital gown. Maybe my exposed bubbles had given the nurse an additional clue of my nakedness.

The nurse flashed me a dirty look and glared at your husband. Her eyes started at his face following the length of him down to the tent in his pants.

You could see the steam coming off this chick. As a side note to you, I want you to know I believe he is doing her! Why else would she have been so angry?

The nurse offered to stay to assist him but he dismissed her. She was not a happy woman as she left my curtained room. She pulled the makeshift wall so violently, I thought it was going to fall of the tracks.

Ignoring her departure, the doctor sat down at my side. "Are you sure you are OK?" He reached over and started stroking my hand gently.

Slightly puffing out my bottom lip, I educated him "I'm actually fine. I might be a little sore everywhere but who can say it was from the accident?"

Your husband appeared very pleased.

He stood up and announced he was taking me to a different room.

"Oh, where are we going?"

He turned and made direct eye contact "How about an all over body massage to ease those aches and pains?"

With a devious grin, I replied. "I do have to follow doctor's orders, don't I?"

He expressed that it was necessary towards the health of my recovery. How could I resist?

Wheeling me down the hall, he requested that I lay still and act like a real injured patient. We moved right past the nurse I am certain is banging your husband. All I could see was him giving a quick nod in her direction. Following the exchange, I heard some drawers being slammed really hard.

He stopped before the elevator, pressed the button and we waited. Moments later, the door opened and he wheeled me in.

A current passenger of the elevator started speaking to your husband "Hey Doc, how ya doing?" He replied he was doing great.

"How's the old lady?"

Don't you just hate when men say that? Your husband relayed to him that you sure are old and very much the same. Nice husband you have there, maybe he should have married younger than himself. I wanted to smack him for you!

The elevator beeped and we lost our ride companion.

"Hey beautiful, are you up for some great hands-on loving?" He slid his hand under my sheet and cupped one of my natural balloons.

"Looking forward to it Doctor, just make me well".

I moistened my lips and inquired as to where he was taking me. He said it was a surprise. Heck, I love surprises!

We jumped off the ride a few seconds later, the elevator door closing behind us.

He whispered "Be really still, I am going to cover you up all the way and pretend you're supplies." The wheels on the gurney need to be oiled desperately.

I had no issues hiding. In fact, I felt as if we were on some kind of an adventure!

Before long, I heard a door open. I was pushed in and the door closed. He had taken the sheet off my head but it was pitch black. I couldn't see anything. This only added an additional layer of excitement to the endeavor.

He didn't want anyone to know we were in there, which was the reason why the lights stayed off. He left me for a moment, he had to get some lotion to rub me down but he would be right back.

I was looking forward to his return because I was FREEZING! Have you ever noticed the climate in hospitals? Institutions are always so damn cold!

He returned a moment later. Dousing his hands with the lotion, he had started to apply it to my body. It was cold at first but my skin quickly warmed it up. He had a magical touch and lover fingers.

Your husband started at my feet, the soles of them and proceeded to my toes. He worked on my calves, thighs and buttocks. My pelvis, abs, breast, back..., OK are you getting the point on how he rubbed every inch of me? He even massaged my face!

He did not miss any part of my torso with the lotion rubdown. I was so relaxed, it was very therapeutic. Better than any massage I had ever received.

I was pretty hot, his hands covered me everywhere. Your husband was pretty excited himself so he ended up telling me "Screw the fact we might get caught! ", he wanted to see me completely naked.

He was thoughtful enough to get an eye mask for me so I would not be blinded by the new contrast. I appreciated the gesture; I really enjoyed the roaming hands in the dark.

"Wow" he said "You are perfect!"

I thanked him and asked your boy what he wanted me to do for him in return?

I did already have sex once that day. Without a shower, I did not want to engage again but I did want to return the favor. I declared to him I was only willing to taste his freezer pop.

He happily agreed and said he would love it! Since I was still lying down on the bed, he just climbed on to the gurney, kneeled above my breasts and then he inserted his Italian ice in my mouth.

That was an enormous gift for me because I did not have to be on my knees. I was a little banged up because my jaw was sore. He said he understood and to just stay really still, keep my mouth open and he would do all the work.

He was moaning away when the door slammed open. A security guard walked in and caught him on top of me while I was still in the process of melting the treat between my lips.

I ripped off the eye mask to see the horrified look on the guard's face. The doc told the man, "Oh come on, like your boat has never rowed its way to the shore here at your work before?"

His response was "Not like this lady!"

I sat up, studied the room and it registered why it was so cold. We were in the Morgue!

Disgusted, I looked down to try and locate a sheet and, in the process, noticed my skin was painted a pale stark white. All of my skin! I jumped up and found a mirror to discover my entire body, including my face, was painted.

No wonder the guard was having stroke, he thought I was dead!

The hospital called the police; they placed your husband in cuffs and led me outside to a waiting police car. Lady, your husband is really, really messed up in the head!

Flabbergasted for awhile, Take Half and Run!
The Other Woman

Cecilia

Dear Cecilia,

I met your husband last night.....

What a strange day I had. I am still walking around in shock over this doctor I met who enjoyed screwing fake dead people. I told you it was a bizarre day! Some secret fantasies individuals have should never be lived out in real life.

I remember this guy who could only get his ship to sail if he wore a pirate's hat.

This man was involved in an accident at some point in his life and he lost one of his hands.

The doctors gave him a choice between a wooden hand and a metal type hook one. He chose the hook because it was more functional.

Now that his physical image had changed, he just couldn't get it up anymore. I believe still to this day that as a child, he was a fan of Captain Hook.

Once he started wearing the hat, he was able to get his boat out of the dock. Soon after, his sex life returned to normal.

One night, while living out some scene from a book of the High Seas, he imagined the girl with him was a treasure chest. He covered her in chains and a pad lock.

In his mind, she was holding all of the gold. He planned on claiming it.

Anyway, in his exhilaration to open the lock on her chest, he swung his altered hand and hooked the poor girl.

I guess those things are pretty sharp! He is now serving twenty-five to life. Like I said, some sexual fantasies are better off not being lived out.

Then there is the story about the guy who was such a golf nut. He had snuck his lady out onto the course after it was closed. He pulled out his nine iron and had her bend over.

He had put the club between his legs and he was just swinging away screaming "Fore", he had to adjust his stance because he really wanted to make a hole in one.

Finally it worked; he could hear fireworks in the distance.

The stupid man did not realize it was a storm he actually heard a bolt of lightning flashed from the sky and made contact with the club shaft. Both of them were fried instantly.

She might have survived if the club was not still in her at the time! The things people do to spice up their love lives.

About your husband, he looked great in uniform. He was the officer who came and picked me up from the hospital and happened to be the cop from my accident site.

When I was escorted to your husband's car, a huge smile of recognition flashed over him. He was very happy to see me. He also glanced down looking for my kitty.

I had purred in his ear while he helped me get in. Sitting in the back of the squad car, I had given him quite the view. I did have my dress back on at the time but still no panties. He was not disappointed.

Your boy certainly was not shy. Most men would try to sneak peeks but not yours. He would look straight between my legs, no cover for him. Even when I adjusted myself on the seat, he actually moved one of my legs back over because they were too close together.

As we pulled away, he turned to me "I can't believe you let that guy paint you." I then had to tell the story of how I did not know the doctor was doing that to me at the time.

I am not sure if he believed me or not. I asked him where we're going and he said "I was told to take you home." Right! Forgot, I still didn't have a car.

During the drive I inquired about you. He explained to me that you were a cutie when the two of you first met and then after a couple of kids, you were spreading in width each year to match the age of your children.

He also informed me that when you two engage in intercourse, he keeps his eyes open. The image of you excites him.

He loved the weight you put on. He never wanted you to diet. Rail-thin women remind him of skeletons, he has no interest in them. I was somewhat surprised and, frankly, I must agree with him. I would never want a rail-thin man, why would men want bony women? Unless, of course, you're an orthopedic physician, then you might get something out of it.

Mr. Cop said, once while having sex and you were on top, he thought his penis was going to explode like a water balloon. The pressure increased the blood flow to his joy toy. Your husband said the feeling it brings is incredible.

There had been some problems a couple of times. One example he gave me was when you placed your hands flat on his chest while riding him and then attempted to balance on your feet, you crushed his chest. He lost his breath and for a moment thought he was dying. He decided he enjoyed asphyxiation and fired his gun into his target.

As any wife would be, you are concerned about his safety. Since then, you are a little shy about mounting him. Trying different positions, he now acts like the new sheriff in town and brings up the rear.

More times than not, you just bend over. He adores your butt. The bigger the better is his opinion. It was nice to hear the statement from a white man.

I was pleasantly astounded by your husband. Most men are such jerks about weight gain but your husband was different. He appreciated your beauty. Many women portray the impression of old artwork; it was sexy to be voluptuous then! You are one of them.

He was bragging he was pretty large down there but, because of the size of your rump and the distance it takes to get his rifle in, only the tip actually enters.

He feels he is not giving you enough satisfaction. He is disappointed about the way insertion has to take place. It causes a lot of air flow to move about.

While having sex, your body begins to play a musical tune which is not very sexy. The location of the sound streaming from your body is not coming from the same area your mans would. Diagnosis; "Female **V**aginal **G**as **S**yndrome."

You are embarrassed and soon just walk away from the love session. I want you to know it happens to all of us girls! We just may not talk about it, nor do I recall "VGS" as a topic of daytime talk shows. A female embarrassing oddity.

I'm not sure how air can get trapped up there and, to this day, no one has made a gas medication to help relieve those types of symptoms. We can only chuckle and try to get back into the mood.

I was pretty surprised he was sharing such a personal story with me.

Changing topics, we spoke about the differences in females. Large, small, tall, short. Somehow native women entered our conversation. We have all seen those clips of villages. Women have bone rings in their noses and their chests look as if they have been sucked dry.

Of course they have been! There is hardly any food over there. Even the men suckle on them for nutrition. Many people are under the assumption it is because villagers do not wear bras. I often wonder if the women live longer than the men in those countries because of where ladies might find protein.

Anyway, he continued by telling me one of your greatest assets is your chest. He is able to place his head between your pillows and you are able to cover him up. It makes him feel as if his mother is swaddling him all over again.

We arrived at my home; he escorted me in. He really was very depressed over you not getting satisfied. He found a book on one of my shelving units. Titled "Loving My Reflection" he asked if he could have it. I told him "Yes".

Still touring my home, he stumbled across an area I have roped off with red velvet. There is a sign posted which states "Admission Is Required". He asked me how much was it?

I replied "What?"

He said "The Admission."

"Oh! I'm sorry you misunderstood; the admission is not a price but a secret. You have to make an admission of truth on any subject and then you may enter."

"See that note pad with the devil on it?" I pointed to the table next to the sign.

"Yes." He replied looking very confused.

"Write your admission/confession on the slip and drop it in the lion's mouth." I pointed out the lion statue that's mouth was open as if it was frozen in a roar.

"What do you do with the admissions?" he answered and started writing.

"Nothing yet, maybe one day I'll write a book". I winked.

He finished, dropped the slip into the lion's mouth and walked beyond the red rope. What he found was another room of my home. My personal playground.

He noticed the sex swing immediately. Your husband peeked around the room admiring all of the other really cool devices. He touched the mink lined cuffs suspended from chains coming down from the ceiling. He patted the top of my mechanical bull while raising a brow in my direction. I could only put both hands up as if saying in sign language "And your point is, what? "

He was very inquisitive about the swing and wanted to know how it worked. I was kind enough to show him. I sat down and raised my legs so I could place them in each strap on the sides. When I had the house built, my plans included reinforced beams.

While I was getting situated he gave me some sob story about you two not having sex for so long which is why he asked me if I would demonstrate this cool device. What the two have to do with the other, I'm not sure. But I am a good host; I played along. I really needed a shower, I told him we could act it out but that was all.

He dropped his pants and I busted out laughing. It was not the size of your butt which was prohibiting you from feeling only the tip. Your husband looked like a banana that someone had peeled and already eaten ninety percent of. Blaming your butt was a joke. This guy could have been female. You poor girl! Why are you with him? At least you were blessed with fingers, longer than your husband's member I might add. Enclosing a penis pump. Maybe it can help him and you.

xoxo The Other Woman

"Wash It From Me"

JOURNAL

Dear Diary,

Finally, the day is over. What an adventure that was. I find people very interesting. Being known as somewhat of a people watcher I am intrigued by human nature. Both sexes have accomplished amazing things, plus some really stupid ones.

Sit-coms are popular because they allow us the opportunity to laugh at ourselves. There is no better medicine then a good belly roar. I certainly had a couple of those today.

Thanking the builder once more for my shower head, any normal water pressure just is not going to get this paint off my body. To explain how thick it is, even my hicky arrow is not showing through.

Getting the water temperature right, I drop the dress and step in. Oh, that feels so good. I reach up and change the setting to a pulsating action. The pressure is so hard that, as the paint is dripping off of my skin, red marks are now showing underneath.

I do like a little pain with my pleasure. As the arrow is starting to appear, I observed it has already started to fade.

Putting body wash on a cloth, I begin soaping myself from head to toe. It's funny that when people are in the shower, our minds slip into some weird zone. Often times we conjure up our best ideas. Many millionaires started with good bathing. My mind is not thinking about money or the newest invention. I can only think about my car. My bag is still in the trunk and I have letters in there which need to make it to the post office.

Turning off the shower and grabbing my towel, I begin the exercise of drying. As to not stretch or wrinkle my skin, I dry in a patting movement.

Finishing that task, I seize my lotion. Although it may be my own hands rubbing my skin, I find pleasure in it. Always starting at the top, my graceful neck is now moisturized, down my shoulders to my breasts. Making a circular motion around each one and ending with pinching the nips. Trailing down the rest of me, lifting each leg and placing a foot on the side of the tub. A stimulating, therapeutic exercise.

When I was married, this was a nightly show for my husband. At the end, we would jump in the sack together. Ok, so I do have some fond memories of the jerk.

Getting dressed again, but this time in a lace negligee, I poured myself a glass of wine and headed to the house phone.

I dialed the police department to speak to the detective regarding my car. The officer told me where I could find it but before hanging up, he said "That Doctor really is an interesting character!"

I replied, "You would never think people could be so strange."

The detective continued "Apparently the nurse he works with..."

Of course I immediately knew which one he was talking about.

"....she was so upset with his arrest and the fact he was with you, she dressed herself in a hospital gown, painted herself white and came to the station."

"She was so obsessed with this guy; she walked in the lobby of the station and demanded she see the doc. When we had to tell her he was not allowed visitors, she threw herself down on the ground and started screaming over and over again; "I would have done that for you, all you had to do was ask!""

It was difficult to hear him clearly through his hysteria.

"The nurse was frenzied at that point. We had to call the hospital and they came to pick her up. She was admitted to the psych ward." He was still drowning himself in laughter.

I could picture tears rolling down his cheeks, him holding his gut with one hand and the phone with the other.

I am laughing so hard myself my side hurt. "Officer, thank you for making the balance of my day." With that, I disconnected the call.

The impound lot was closed for the evening, so making any calls would not result in anything. I was whooped. Taking the final sip of my wine, I retired to my bedroom.

Early the next morning, I pick up my car and head to the dealership for repairs. Boy, I'm so excited - Not!

Before I sign off for the evening, I have to touch base on the wife who demanded her husband listen, clean up and follow orders.

If someone's husband was lazy or sexist when they first met them, why do women think these guys will change? They don't and won't. I believe before anyone ever gets married, they should draft a contract which lays out the terms of the marriage. Such as:

New Husband: don't expect me to clean or cook. I will play golf every weekend. When my sports teams are on television, I expect you to shut up and don't ever think I am not playing baseball or re-enrolling on the bowling league.

The New Wife: It's in my blood to nag because that is what my mother did. I will shop until we have to file bankruptcy and after I have kids don't even think you are getting laid more than once every couple of weeks and that's if you are lucky.

Wives are just replacements for moms. Trust me - these moms are happy to pass the torch.

Sweet Dreams.

Courtney

Dear Courtney,

I met your husband last night.....

When a woman needs work done to her auto, the first thing that enters the mind of these grease monkeys at the repair shop is "Hurray, I can screw her!" I don't mean in the physical sense but by way of pocket book.

Mechanics presume ladies are so stupid they can take advantage of us. It's a shame really. Used car salesmen get such a bad rap, when in my book these guys are on the top of the "Bend over this won't hurt, I promise" theory. It's always painful!

As a girl, I will agree I have no idea how a car actually works. All I need to know is you put gas in and turn the key. Then when I am at the wheel and guiding it, I make it go to my destination.

Technology has even made it simpler for us. On some new cars you can just push a button and presto, your car is running. Maybe a class action suit was brought against the car engineers for carpal tunnel damage. Thus, the push button was born.

We are almost better off hiring a man to be a "Car Repair Agent" for us gals. If the male species is involved, the price is certain to be lower!

A girl can go in and get a quote from a repair thief, then send the "Repair Agent" to another location. Many are franchises; they are believed to do their estimates from the computer. At least that is what we are told.

After both quotes are complete, take the two estimates, find the difference and split it in two. Even though you are not getting the lowest price, you are still saving a ton of money! I have now created a job for your friends who have an unemployed husband. This may equate to about one half. Maybe the lazy slobs will get off the couch and release the death hold on the clicker. It has all the perfect ingredients for them: money, women and cars.

As you know your husband owns a local car dealership with a repair shop. I was involved in a car accident and I had the impound lot tow my baby over to his place of business.

I have an idea you already know who I am at this juncture. My reputation is getting around and many wives are afraid to see the postman.

I can picture you walking to your box, stopping with hesitation. Your pulse rate picks up because of the anxiety you are feeling. Dread is such a terrible feeling, is it not? The only reason why you feel this way is because you have a sinking feeling in the pit of your stomach; you know your husband is a bad boy. You just happen to be one of those wives who do not want to admit it. Time to be confronted with the truth.

Ignoring all of the clues left around you, being blind on purpose. Some women are just plain stupid, not you. You are very smart!

You live in a beautiful six-bedroom home, never having to work a day in your life. A stressful afternoon might be shopping, lunch, nails and cocktails.

If you had to face reality, you might have to give up this world you live in. As happy as I am for you living in your fantasy world, there is something you need to know.

If you can still stick by him after knowing everything I am about to tell you, that's your decision. I am only the messenger.

Finally, on this day, you take a deep breath, pull down the door to your mailbox and you find my letter.

Are you wondering why the envelope is black? I find females are more logical. We tend to see things in black and white, while men, in their delusional state of mind, only seem to see things in color.

This is one of the main differences between the sexes. If your husband had to open the mailbox, he wouldn't even see the letter from me. I take advantage of this chromosomal flaw and men's arrogance. It's perfect for me because this letter is meant for you!

Arriving at the dealership, I noticed they have one of those machines which dispense numbered slips of paper. Most customers are already trained in walking over and pulling one of those things free from the machine.

They look up at the LCD screen and see forty other numbers before them. Cursing to themselves, they walk to the waiting area, sit down, pick up a magazine and settle in for a long day. I have no patience for that. I inquired where the owner was.

The blond chickie at the desk attempted to give me some excuse he was tied up and not able to see anyone. Smiling, I excused myself and went in search of his office. I never take no for an answer.

The building is very large and spacious. There are hallways and conference rooms galore, filled with sales people dressed to impress and customers excited about signing on the bottom line. I have no idea why, considering when they drive their new car from the lot, five thousand dollars just dropped out of the trunk on the road.

I stuck my head in just about everywhere when I finally found a door that was marked "Private".

Why bother knocking when I am intruding anyway. I opened the mahogany door and strolled right in. There before my eyes was a drop dead gorgeous office. Your husband has great taste.

The room colors were a muted beige and eggshell. Beautiful paintings covered most of the walls. On his desk, I found a picture of the two of you. You are striking!

He had two matching camel color leather couches. There was even an entire wall that was an aquarium. Some of the fish seemed to be as large as football? They were all different tropical species. I even discovered a seahorse in his mini-ocean!

The only person in the room was me. Your husband was missing in action. Making myself comfortable, I removed my heels and melted on a couch.

I was truly mesmerized by those fish. It appeared one of them was in heat; she was running around all over the tank and was sought after by five other ones. I guessed those ones to be the boys.

All breeds of life are the same. I chuckle to myself that maybe the female fish should just stop swimming and have an orgy with the gents.

Then it occurred to me. Maybe she was running away because she did not want to get pregnant. Yep, I doubt there is fish birth control mixed in with the food. Your husband would want her to get pregnant to fill his tank even further. I was very tempted to get her out of there!

A noise suddenly brought me back to why I was there.

What was that sound? It was very mottled. Standing and putting my shoes back on, I walked over to the door and opened it. Glancing into the hallway, I found no signs the noise was coming from out there.

Closing the door again, I strained to hear what direction it was coming from. I circled his office to locate the source of the sound. It resembled moaning. I soon discovered it was coming from behind the wall of book shelves.

I walked back into the hallway to see if I could find a door to the adjoining room. Nothing. Back into his office again.

On one of the shelves there was a statue of a naked woman. It was rather pretty. She looked like a goddess. I tried picking it up but it was permanently attached to the shelf.

Interestingly enough, the arm above her head moved a little. Pulling her arm down, it reaches her naked groin. Her fingers were extended from her hand so when her limb was in a lower position, it actually entered a hole there.

I quickly appreciated whoever's imagination had made the piece of art. To my surprise a moment later, I heard a click and one of the book case units slightly became ajar. Wow, how cool was that?

I pulled the case open and found a circular staircase. Candle operas on the walls lit my path to the top. Upon entering the second story, I was in shock and delighted as to what I discovered.

It was an adult playground headquarters. Erotic music was echoing softly throughout the room. To my right there was a large marble jet tub. It was on, the water was bubbling and steam was rising from it.

In front of me there was a platform with a beautiful shiny pole coming out of it and made its way to the ceiling. Your husband had his very own stripper pole!

Making a mental note to get one of these installed at my home, I discover the floor of the platform was all mirrors. I was so taken away by this; I stopped my mission to try it out.

I removed all of my clothing, except my stilettos and stepped onto the stage. Grabbing the pole with my hand, I swung around and then wrapped my legs around it.

Keeping to the beat of the music, I found myself using my imagination and so I began making love to the pole. I could still hear the moaning, the sound only added to my excitement!

While sliding myself down the steel rod, it was rubbing against me. I was able to climax just as my bottom was in full view of the mirror below. I watched myself tremble. That was fun!

Judging me? Had you known it was up there, you would have done the same thing yourself. Most women have fantasized about being a dancer and many have danced for their men. Ok, so I did this for me but it was the mirror on the floor got me going. Maybe I have a mirror fetish? I'll continue now.

Dressing myself, I went back to the mission at hand. Where was the sound coming from?

I walked in another doorway and discovered a television screen covering an entire wall. Your husband sure liked everything big!

The monitor was playing a video of your husband engaged in a sexual act. It appeared he has a preference for younger men. I do have to admit, his partner was a hunk; I judged him to be in his late twenties.

I glanced to the other side of the room and finally discovered the source of the sound.

Your man was hog-tied on a circular bed. Tears rolled down his face. He was naked and a wad of paper was shoved in his mouth.

In the horror of seeing me, he began hyperventilating and then passed out. I was certain the lack of air supply and his struggling helped create his new medical condition.

I removed the paper from his mouth and opened it up. It was a picture of the young man on the screen with the girl from the repair desk. She did not lie after all when she said your husband was *tied up*!

Scorned women can be so brutal. I wondered how long she would have left him that way. Maybe she wanted her boyfriend to find him. I thought it was comical she was working away, just like any other day!

Slapping him back to conscientiousness, your husband and I had chitchat. I agreed to untie him and he agreed to fix my car for free. He also made me promise I would not tell anymore. I am happy to report my fingers were crossed behind my back.

On this occasion I did not need an Auto Repair Broker for myself. Who could beat the price of free?

Get the Strip Pole in the divorce!

Very Truly Sorry For You,
The Other Woman

"Dating Instruction Guide"

JOURNAL

Dear Diary,

How funny was that? I think this was the one and only time I had to take a picture with my camera phone of someone's husband. Yep, you guessed it. I plugged my phone into my computer and presto; a cute pic of hubby tied up. Of course I had to send it with the letter.

I don't understand a couple things. Why get married if you're gay? I have a lot in common with gay men. A couple examples would be: we both like men and adore those little yellow cakes with cream filling. Also gay men and I love the back door entrance and to be mounted. These guys have a better sense of style and they make better friends than the female counterpart. They never get jealous or borrow your clothes and never return them.

Getting back to the married thing; is it really fair to the woman? Don't be shy! Get out of the closet, the door has been opened now for many years. Gay men no longer need a cover to hide behind. Take a look at the political scandals. Stupid really; be honest!

Why do men never consider us? I am sure the husband sucked in bed, give the wife a break and let her find something which satisfies her hunger. Maybe she would have been interested in joining them. You never know?! Some couples do have open marriages. Better known as Swingers.

Life would be so much easier if men could be rubber stamped at birth. Since they are not, I developed the below chart to help women of the world identify men. All girls would need to do is take each letter from their man's name and match it up with my chart. Let's take a guy named Frank as an example.

Frank in my experience is:

*ucked up in the head, acts retarded, is an asshole, very much a nerd; however he is kind of kinky.

A is for Asshole
B is for in-Breeding or potential thereof
C is for Cheater
D is for Dork
E is for Electrifying in Bed
F is for *ucked Up!
G is for Giant Penis
H is for Hermit
I is for Inmate
J is for Juvenile Personality
K is for Kinky
L is for Liar and Lazy
M is for Mommy's Boy
N is for Nerd
O is for Obstetrician (or OB wanna be's)
P is for Partier
Q is for Queer
R is for Rapper (or droopy drawers)
S is for Sex Offender
T is for Tight Wad
U is for Ugly
V is for Vehicle Parked on Lawn
W is for Welfare

X is for X Rated Personality
Y is for Yuppie
Z is for Zoo Keeper let him out

Presto, dating made easy. I have taken the guess work out of it! Does anything else really need to be said?

Time to dream. Tomorrow I have a charity event to attend.

Good Night.

Alexa

Dear Alexa,

I met your husband last night.....

I was at a charity funds raiser and your husband was in attendance. A live auction was scheduled for the evening's entertainment. The auctioneers were not raffling off items; instead, the crowd would be bidding on dates.

All of the women up for sale were stunning! The men could hardly contain themselves. The guest count for this private affair was exactly enough girls on stage for the gentleman in attendance.

The facility rented for this occasion was inside that brand new hotel downtown. All of the mattresses are down-filled. The bedding is made of the highest thread count, making you feel like you slipped into a bed of pudding. The tubs are located on the balconies of each room with a mesh screen which rolls down for those needing privacy. All of the towels are in a warming unit and the floors are heated.

The rooms are digital and respond to verbal commands. Each room allows you to order a virtual date (male or female) that can appear as a hologram. If you close your eyes, you can almost feel them touching you. The virtual data runs off of some mega computer somewhere and its vocabulary is unlimited. They act in a servant capacity, so your wish is its command.

I Met Your Husband Last Night

I admit it; I had already stayed in that hotel. I figured out how to order multiple virtual dates, an orgy happening in my room without risk of disease. Sex of the future is now here!

Before the auction process started, the men were able to mingle with the girls. Lots of alcohol was being served. The goal was to raise one million dollars that night. The flowing booze loosened up the wallets of the men and women.

I was one of those dates being sold off. Before you make judgment, it was for charity. I can assure you this was a first experience for me but I had so much fun I guarantee you I will do it again.

The dates had to enter the stage so the bidding war could begin. The audience was at attention. Their eyes glued on the candy they desired.

The speaker called each girl by their first name to take center stage. She was asked to tell the crowd what she desired most out of a man. Because the object was to raise as much money as possible with bids, the answers ranged from...

"having a man allow me to be submissive...let me watch him with another woman...anal sex...letting me give him blow jobs hourly...having sex with me and another woman...letting me only wear lingerie whenever in doors..." Of course my answer was only "wearing stilettos twenty four seven".

I believe the girls answered in a manner which every man desired to hear!

At the end of the interview session, each lady had to turn a 360 and strut down the catwalk. Hips were swaying and breasts a- bouncing.

You may have been to an auction before or maybe you have seen one broadcasted. Each person is given a number to represent them. When they make a bid, they hold up their number printed on a piece of paper. Our charity organizer was very clever, as each number was printed on a cardboard type of stock, but also cut out in the shape of a penis. From the stage's perspective, it was an interesting sight to see all those penises bopping up and down in the air. If you had no idea what was actually going on, you may have thought it was a dick convention.

I was so nervous about having the highest bidder be some dork. When it was my turn, I apparently had the interest of a handful of guys. A couple of them really old, some bald, some not, some cute and a couple dogs. But one of them was smoking hot. I had smiled in his direction, winked and touched my chest. I was beyond excited when they announced your husband had won me.

Strolling to the stage, he was as proud as a peacock. Your guy did an excellent job outbidding the rest of the men for me. He approached the event organizer and handed in his check. Then it was time for him to collect his trophy.

Extending me his hand, he had helped me exit the stage.

When we hugged, I was sure to move my pelvis in and apply just enough pressure to gauge my own prize. I was equally satisfied.

We had walked over to a quiet corner, escaping some of the madness. Bidding was still in session.

He informed me that he was almost divorced. In my opinion, "almost" counts. He had called a limo service to pick us up about an hour later. As he disconnected his call, he had glanced behind me and a hors d'oeuvre table captured his attention.

He had picked up a chocolate-covered strawberry and brought it gently to my lips. I had licked around it as if it was a lollypop before nibbling off a bite.

Moving closer to him, I had tilted my face towards his and he tilted down. Our lips met with passion and desire. Our tongues danced together and I shared my nibble. It was a very tasty kiss. Beside the sweetness to it, I could also taste the testosterone raging through his beautiful body. Has that ever happened with you?

We danced and mingled with the other guests for the duration of our stay. Many of the new couples had headed upstairs to those incredible rooms I had told you about. We instead walked outside to our waiting driver.

At curbside, a sparkling clean white limo waited. The driver had opened the rear door; your husband and I slid onto the white leather seats. I had chuckled to myself that white may not have been a suitable color, for our evening was going to be far from pure.

The first thing your husband did was put up the divider between the back and front seat. Popping the cork on the champagne and stripping at the same time is quite the feat. Did you know your husband was so talented?

So there was your naked man, sitting proud in all of his glory. The stake between his legs was standing straight up, silently screaming..." Hello, look at me!"

Have you ever noticed the tip of a man's circumcised penis resembles a helmet? On some men, even a mushroom. The first penis I had ever witnessed live scared me. I screamed and ran away. Although his name was Steve, to my friends he was now known as the Mushroom Man. It took years for me to get over the image. Well, maybe I didn't since I'm writing to you about it. However, I have since matured and *swallowed* its interesting design.

It was a very cool evening; I was freezing in my little dress and had to turn on the heat in the limo. Of course it did not last long; we created enough heat between the two of us, I ultimately had to turn the heat off.

Your husband enjoyed removing my clothing. I luxuriated in letting him. Remember when you first started dating your husband? All he had to do was brush by you and you would be soaking wet? Does that still happen? Of course it doesn't! Miss it, don't you?

The windows fogged up and the bumps in the car only made the pounding more intense. I am trying to not be too explicit for you but I need to get my point across. Stretch limousines have terrible shocks but for what we were doing, it was a perfect compliment.

We traveled all over the city, I am sure the driver was dying to know what was actually going on in the back of his car.

Careful not to damage the mirrors in the roof of the car, I removed my stiletto heels. Whoever came up with the idea of reflections in the ceilings of these cars was a genius. It's essentially like having sex and watching porn at the same time!

We opened the sunroof and somehow we both fit our bodies through the opening. He was behind me. Hanging onto the top of the car for leverage and standing on the interior seats, we managed to engage in intercourse inside and outside of the car.

The fellow travelers on the road that evening surely could tell by the expressions on our face, what was taking place below the roofline. Many of those other drivers may have been disappointed the windows were tinted. I know I would have been.

Dropping back in the limo onto the seat, I felt something pulsating on my butt cheeks. At first, I thought maybe this hotel room on wheels came with vibrating seats, but then I heard a chirping sound.

Your husband's phone was ringing. He did not answer it. Ok, he was ignoring it. Champagne was poured into my mouth, overflowing it trickled down my neck between my perky breasts, past my flat stomach and dripped from my happy zone, right into your husband's mouth. Glasses are so overrated!

The telephone rang again, once more he ignored it. On the third call he finally turned to me and said "I need to take this." Not a problem.

This is pretty close to his phone conversation.

"Hello?"

Please remember I was only getting one side of the chat session.

"Oh, Hi Honey!" he settled back into his seat.

"Yeah, I went with Bob."

"No, you don't need to worry about me being home for dinner, I ate out."

I thought to myself, yes he sure did! Your husband then looked at me with an expression that resembled guilt.

"No, Bob left already; I had to swing by the office."

"Uh, no, I am actually in the storage room, I did hear the office line ring but I am knee deep in boxes."

"I will be home later."

"I love you too." He pushed (end) on his cellular phone.

He apologized for the interruption. I could not help but say to him "That's a pretty pleasant conversation for someone who's almost divorced."

He smiled, pulled me on his lap and replied "That's because it was my daughter."

Congratulations on almost being single,
The Other Woman

"Emotions Running High"

JOURNAL

Dear Diary,

I must admit I had a great time tonight. The theme about bidding on dates was very cute, but I feel it's more of a theory than a theme. Girls are possessions to men; many times they purchase the woman they desire with gifts. Men never want to lose them once they have them, even if they don't want her anymore. What I mean is this; it's OK for the man to walk away but never the woman.

Sometimes men never get over the fact they did lose the broad. Instead of these idiots figuring out it happened because their behaviors were stupid, they choose to place blame on the girl. Men forget they cheated, were never at home, and treated their girls like a piece of furniture, beat them and/or degraded them.

I guess stalking situations can happen with both sexes. Many times they can turn violent. Property damage, threats, unexpected visits. Violence is a major problem in some relationships. I'm all into whips and chains on occasion, but don't ever hit me.

Jealously is also a dangerous emotion. Remember the chick that cut off her hubbie's "stubby"? Then she drove it miles down the road and threw it out the window like the trash that it was.

I joined her fan club. You go girl!

Daisy

Dear Daisy,

I met your husband last night.....

Earlier in the week I was without transportation for a couple of days. Taking advantage of the downtime, I worked from home.

I had never been a big fan of renting cars. I have a clean fetish and just thinking about someone else's dirty rump having been on the seat I am sitting on disgusts me.

Besides finding the seats repulsive in rentals, I just about throw up at the thought of the steering wheel. Yuck!

Why on earth do many people not wash their hands after exiting the restroom? Once, a guy friend and I were having dinner. After each visit he made to the bathroom, he would point out the other males who did not wash up after yanking on their pee pees. I asked him not to do that anymore because I lost my appetite after looking over at someone he pointed out and the guy was eating chicken wings. My friend told me he washes before and after urinating. He couldn't stand the thought of touching his own penis with dirty hands.

I personally find public restrooms a cesspool of disease. But when you gotta go, you gotta go.

When I find myself in that situation, I place tissue on the seat cover and stoop, bending my knees and hovering at least a foot away.

I have plastic covers that go over my shoes also. I flush the toilet with my shoe, open the turn lock with tissue in my hand, walk to the sink and wash my hands, always using another paper towel to actually turn the water back off.

I grab the door handle with the towel and use my hip to hold the stall door open while playing basketball to toss my used tissues in the trash.

Using a plastic bag I collect from the market, I put my hand inside, reach to the bottom and use it almost like a glove.

Removing the plastic on my shoes, and I pull the bag inside out, as to not touch the booties. Yes, even women manage to pee on the floor. Sorry, I am a little off topic, my mind wonders often.

Back to that day's events.

Getting ready for the evening, I picked a simple black dress. Low-cut and form fitting.

If I decide to wear hose, it is usually the kind with the piping up the back of the calf; sexy!

My shoes are always stilettos and five inches high. It has taken many years to walk gracefully in them. I wear a variety of colors, always matching my evening's outfit.

Scanning the newspaper earlier, I noticed there was a wonderful blues band playing at the bar down by the water. You know the one your husband takes you for your birthday every year and special occasions.

It is a third-generation family Italian restaurant "Sam's Place". Don't let the name fool you, it's a fantastic restaurant! Red velvet drapes from the ceiling of the main bar with every possible type of liquor you could desire. There is the standing unspoken rule the wives are only allowed to dine there on Saturday nights. If one of the regulars is foolish enough to bring his wife on a Friday, the staff will escort out other husbands and their mistresses through the back door.

A look of understanding on your face, perhaps? Yes, that is why your husband only takes you there on Saturday nights.

Patty, my favorite bartender of all time, keeps everyone at an even keel. She is not only gorgeous but she holds everyone's dirty little secrets. If anyone could write a book, she could. But that's not her nature. Playing barkeep, minister and psychologist is not for everyone. She handles it with grace and discreetness.

This night happened to be a Friday, so the odds were that, there should be no wives present. Although most of the men would already have a date with them, there are the ones who do come alone. This is an upscale restaurant; the food + drink prices are high. Having this type of atmosphere attracts the highly paid hookers. Presto, a solution for gentlemen to visit unaccompanied. They never leave that way.

I walked in and strutted to the bar area, waiving hello to Patty in the process. The restaurant had recently expanded to include a deck outside. It was pretty hopping. Handsome men and beautiful women, all dressed to the nines. An electrifying environment!

Sitting alone at one of the tables was a breathtaking female. That is saying a lot coming from me. I ordered a drink and viewed the crowd but my eyes kept roaming back to the lovely creature a few feet away from me.

She had a full mane of blonde hair and long eyelashes. From a distance, her eyes may have been green. Her face looked as if an artist chiseled it to perfection. She had high cheekbones and a long sexy neck. She was tan but not too dark. Just perfect, everything about her was perfect. Her breasts peeked out of the top of her form fitting shirt; they were bulging and wanted to be released.

She raised her drink, inviting me to join her. Heck, why not?

As I approached the table, the waiter had already pulled my seat out for me. Gazing down, I could see her muscular calves connecting to sexy feet. Stilettos attached. Meow!

She clinked her glass to mine and told me her name was Destiny. How fitting! I could already tell she was going to be my final destination for that evening.

During out chit-chat, she informed me she was waiting for someone but also said I would be an added flavor to dinner and hoped I would stay.

Thinking to myself that normally, I am not attracted to females, this one had broken my rules of gender preference.

In walked your husband, also known as the dinner date she was expecting. We were introduced. He was very good looking. I had only expected them to be equally matched in appearance.

He sat down; the waitress had come over to take his drink order. As the conversation made circles around the table, I found myself wandering off in thought of the two of them.

I watched the way he touched her, it was exotic and exciting. He stroked her arm, legs and even the side of her face with such a gentleness and longing. I wished my hand was cupped inside his, so I could feel too.

I asked them if they would prefer to be alone and they answered in the manner I was seeking. His deep sexy voice repeated "No, we like to be watched". Well, that was really hot!

The evening progressed and I did watch. I couldn't help myself. I was turning down men left and right who had approached me for a dance. This couple had my juices flowing; no one else existed that night.

I watched them on the dance floor. He was holding her tight and using his free hand to caress her body. It was beautiful, almost like he was sculpting her.

When they came back to the table for the last time, they announced they we're leaving and asked me if I wanted to join them. I quickly told them "Of Course".

I followed them in my car back to your house. You have a daughter who is in labor out of state and you were not expected to be home for several weeks. Beautiful home by the way. Your husband poured cocktails for the three of us.

He reached for both of our hands and led us to your bedroom. You have a canopy king-size bed and a chaise lounge. The perfect seat to watch the show about to unfold.

He walked her to the bed and guided me to the chase. Getting comfortable, I watched as she slowly undressed your man.

She bit off each button on his dress shirt and exposed a muscular chest underneath. He had strong shoulders and a flat stomach. Just enough hair to not be vulgar.

She enjoyed using her mouth because she was using it to loosen the belt on his pants. She was successful in getting it undone and continued using her teeth to unbutton his slacks and pull down the zipper. She proceeded by swallowing him whole. Wow, she was talented because your boy is not little.

The image of her doing this act created a flashback for me of being a teenager again. My girlfriends and I would practice on bananas. Close your jaw; I am almost certain you did the very same thing.

It was not long before your husband's volcano erupted and they switched positions with each other.

Your husband started removing her clothing. Wearing a sheer blouse and a skirt, he began at the top, the shirt soon came off. He proceeded to remove her bra.

Proof of an expensive surgery for her twins; you could hardly see the scar! She also sunbathes nude, because she had no tan lines.

Destiny eased back in your bed and separated her long tan thighs. Your husband began kissing at her ankle and preceded all of the way up her legs. Instead of removing her skirt, he simply just ducked his head under it.

This beautiful being had continued glancing in my direction to see if I was still watching. She smiled in delight to see I was.

Come on, I couldn't get my eyes off those two if the house was on fire!

His head was barely exposed but through her skirt I could see him moving around. The motion looked as if he was licking ice-cream from a bowl.

I knew the time had come in which he had reached the bottom of his dish and found the cherry. She released and made a sound similar to one which escapes me.

It's comical the expression we make when having an orgasm, it resembles pain.

He rolled off her and she excused herself to the restroom. From where I was sitting, I had a perfect view of the bath and her walking into it. It was erotic to watch her swinging her hips topless, with only the skirt on and stilettos.

Stopping at the mirror first, she combed her fingers through her long mane. Satisfied with her reflection, she turned to walk in the direction of the toilet. Having no desire to close the door, she left it open.

As she lifted her skirt, I enjoyed a view of her hot buns. Wondering to myself if I get to watch another show, in the blink of an eye, she took a leak. Honestly, I was very shocked that I was attracted to her. My conclusion is that I still only like men!

Does He Make You Wear A Strap-On?
The Other Woman

"Building Your Own Version"

JOURNAL

Dear Diary,

I drove away that night thinking how bizarre it is for a man to want to dress as a woman. Is it really some weird cellular thing that gets screwed up when growing in the womb?

She really was a beautiful lady, prettier than most of the female population. Funny how that works!

What I found more disturbing was the husband. If you like guys, then like guys. But why some version of the two sexes?

I am not homophobic. Find happiness where it exists. I don't expect people to understand me, so I won't place judgment upon others. Although, I will always be curious as to the "why's" though.

Men find two women together hot. I find two or more men together <u>with me </u>hot. It's our animal instinct, being a little like a savage sometimes can certainly re-spark a love life.

My problem is not with two men together, two women or an entire colony of people getting it on. My problem is with the wife who does not know, the clueless unsuspecting bride.

If the men could just be honest with their partners for a change, maybe allow the wife some fun as well or, perhaps, the opportunity to leave, then I would not have to write these letters!

I have asked many men, Why they can't just be truthful with their spouses? Their answers vary slightly. But not by much.

I have surveyed and inquired if their wife was out cheating on them, would they have a problem with it? One hundred percent has answered "Yes".

What is up with that? I suppose it goes back once again to those animal instincts. Men pee on us and we belong to them but they are free to roam the land and spray on additional territories and beings.

We can try and blame our creator but no one is forcing us into marriage. Some husbands secretly desire to be woman. They sneak into their wives' closets and wear their undergarments. Really, it happens.

On a different note, I have wondered if the wives receiving my letters appreciate my personal realization and my viewpoint on my various side subjects. The world is just plain weird. Humans act so oddly. I can't be the only person who notices the behavior of our sick society.

I am sleeping better than most. Good Night!

Mia

Dear Mia,

I met your husband last night......

I had been working a lot recently but some personal issues kept me at home. When I did return, the work in my office was piled up everywhere. I was hoping the work I did from home covered it but I was sadly mistaken; they did not e-mail it all to me.

My employer has work stations and offices covering approximately One Hundred Thousand square feet. It's like a mini-city.

We have our own work-out facilities, daycare center and full cafeteria. The theory behind it is, make us happy and we will work harder and better. I believe they just never want us to leave there.

Each work station has a computer. There are more than a thousand people employed at each shift and it runs three shifts daily. Due to the amount of people, we certainly have our fair share of affairs between the employees.

A popular toy to relieve some of the hum-drum in this place is online instant messaging. When you hear a giggle from another station, you know they are chatting with someone.

Thus the office romances and broken marriages begin.

I Met Your Husband Last Night

While I was gone, the company hired someone new in my department. That would be your husband.

His office is conveniently located right next to mine. I only had the opportunity to see him coming and going from lunch from the time I returned to work; until last night

He was and is a dashing man. He has expensive taste and a magic about him that is enticing. He dresses fabulously! A black dress hat and dark sun glasses are set off by an English walking stick. He reminds me of a trip I once had to London. Oh, that is a fond memory.

Your husband is very sure of himself. He had an appealing arrogance; it is very difficult to not notice him. Other men must envy his natural charm.

A month passed by and I could not get your husband to notice me. He comes into work, does his job and leaves. We had never even been formally introduced.

Human nature. To want something we don't have. Desiring it so strongly it can take over our thinking!

Our behavior is primal in nature. The thrill of the chase and hunt. Seeking to capture our prey, to dominate. Many sportsmen hunt deer; they tolerate all kinds of weather conditions. They sleep in the cold and they don't bathe for fear the deer might actually smell them. Some even purchase deer urine and douse themselves with it. Very few, once they kill the prized buck, actually mount the rack or head. By then, the thrill is over. They set out to conquer and win. Mission accomplished.

Many relationships happen the same way. Well, not entirely. Men and women will bathe and won't spread urine on themselves normally. The bottom line being once the hunt is over, the excitement is gone too. And so is mounting the other. Sounds like a lot of marriages I know.

Never had I thought anyone was outside my reach but it appeared your husband was starting to make me have some doubts.

Chatting with some of the other girls at work, they also noticed your hubby. Frankly, I can't think of any female who could not. I had no interest in their petty rejection stories; they did not have all of the talents I do. It only means he has higher standards.

Is it possible your husband did fall into the slim group of men who had sown their wild oats and remained faithful to their wife? So happy at home they do not see or care to take interest in other females?

If that is the case, whatever you have girl; you could bottle and sell it on the black market. You would make a killing!

It also occurred to me maybe you could offer classes "Neuter Your Straying Tom Cat Overnight!" Your classes would be continuously full, with a several-year wait list.

One day, I had seen him in the hallway approaching me. Doing a trick dating back to middle school, I dropped to the file I was holding to the ground.

The shirt I was wearing had my breasts spilling out. Gravity helping, I bent over. He just casually passed me by. I turned around to see if he at least glanced at my perfect buns and he never even bothered to look. Hum.

I couldn't sleep that night. I might have been obsessed with him. I could not get him off of my mind. It was really screwing me up mentally. I'm sure it's still the thrill of the chase, but I had never - I mean never - had this happen before.

So I planned the ultimate thing to do. I would finally meet your husband!

The next day, I brought an overcoat with me to work. It was easier to get through the workday because I knew I was going to conquer him. Your boy did not stand a chance!

Before the day ended, I went into the supply closet, removed all of my clothing and put on the coat. I walked into his office; the stilettos pumping confidently, and shut the door. "Excuse me, I'm sorry to interrupt you."

The sun was setting and the rays were shining onto your husband. There was a halo of light framing him; he almost looked like a god.

He replied "No apology required; how can I help you?"

I proceeded to tell him how happy I was when he joined our company. I was dying to know what his eyes looked like but anyone would have to wear shades to sit in the afternoon sun pouring through his windows.

Taking advantage of the stream of light, I used it as a spotlight. Tired of the repartee and wanting to get down to business, I dropped the overcoat.

His facial expression had not changed at all! Maybe I read this guy wrong. Could he be gay?

Are my senses really that out of whack?

Still standing there still naked, his office door opened. In walked one of the other office guys.

"Holy crap!" His mouth was hanging to the floor.

I spun around to face him, pleased to elicit some kind of response "Thank you, at least you noticed!"

Your husband spoke up and said "Notice what?" If you could have seen the expression on my face, I almost smacked him for that reply!

The office guy began laughing; as he collapsed on the floor in hysteria, he informed me that your husband is blind.

It all makes sense now. Maybe the women who are searching want ads for a husband should follow your path; you have the right idea! It just may keep them from straying.

With My Respect,
The Other Woman

"Equal Rights"

JOURNAL

Dear Diary,

Is that what it takes for a man to not notice a woman? They need to be blind? Driving down the road or out at some public place, men can suffer whiplash looking at women.

Most of us have been given the gift of sight and we should all appreciate beauty before us. But, come on guys, show some decency and do it when your girl is not around.

It's rude and thoughtless.

Then there are the guys who get caught and comment...

"Honey, did you see those big hooters, there is no way they are real!"

I think women should reverse it on them.

"Babe, did you see that guy's huge bulge, I wonder if it's real?"

If we started talking about other men's sexual organs, maybe these dips will get the hint. If not, maybe the wife just located something better. She should go touch it and determine if it's the genuine article.

Hopefully, it will be an easy day at work tomorrow.

Ashlyn

Dear Ashlyn,

I met your husband last night.....

One odd trait most men seem to possess is the natural born instinct to name their attached organ. Why on earth do they do that? We name people and animals, sometimes trucks and boats; often we come up with clever nicknames for friends.

I have never been in a conversation with a woman when she is telling me she needs to use the restroom and uncap her Wet Wanda.

How often have you heard a man use a stupid line like "Hey, gotta go use the john and drain the anaconda"?

Or how about when they think they are being cute and want to sleep with you, a man might may say something like this: " My 'Wet Willy' is looking to take a dip in your lake"?

Maybe it's the mother's fault that men name their penises. At birth, mommy's begin repeating to their little boys, this is your wee-wee. As they grow up (at least in height), the pet name given by the mother is not very masculine. What once was called a wee-wee is now "Humongous Hugo". Maybe the mommies should take the responsibility of this ritualistic behavior.

There is more to this analogy besides naming it; men treat their organ like another human. Often you might find them talking to their penises, giving them encouragement.

Alcohol can play a role in a man's performance in bed. It slows down the blood flow. Men may try convincing their best friend to play along. It may sound something like this "Come on Soldier, I worked all night to get this chick in the sack. I have done my job, now it's up to you. Come on buddy, stand at attention! I need bullets in that rifle; pretend she is the target of a firing squad. Let's blow her apart!" Men are also sympathetic to their "friend" and, while speaking to it, they will stroke it with love.

Sometimes it works, other times it does not. It is disappointing for the girl when it doesn't. Men have yet to figure out while they are sweet talking and coxing their penises, we are getting turned off!

Can you imagine a girl doing that? "Ok, 'Puppy Love', you have never failed me before. Your instinct to smell meat a mile away has always been great; tonight I have brought the feast to you. I'm drooling over this steak, now I need you to do the same!"

Women are just plain smarter. We just open the night stand and pull out the lubricant. Men who say it's not that easy for them speak Hogwash! Big business has created something for them also.

It's called a Rooster Ring. Like a rubber band, it slides over the love toy and traps blood flow in its tracks. Instant erection! It lasts as long as they wear it. In my opinion, Rooster Rings should share space with condoms in bar bathroom vending machines.

Guys additionally have another habit; touching themselves. They tell us it's an itch or they are adjusting themselves. My hypothesis is that men need constant assurance their "friend" is still there.

Where on earth do they think it's going to go? Come on, it's attached to them like a conjoined twin. One is not smarter than the other; they are both equally dumb.

As men age, gravity is not kind to them. They sag just like women. Sometimes it's horrifying. It's Ok for a young guy to wear boxers, just as if it's Ok for a young woman to wear no bra. But as the years pass and are not so kind, older men really should wear briefs for support.

I have witnessed too many older men cupping their nuts and lifting them before sitting. As they are doing this act to save themselves some pain, a young boy is watching. Seeing this behavior begins the circle of tradition. The lad has now been taught that when he is old; to touch, lift and sit. That is how boys are taught to pee standing up. They learn by example.

The moment a wife's breasts begin to sag, her husband is often encouraging her to get a boob job.

Why has our medical community not come out with the "Macadamia to Peanuts Overnight" surgery for the old dudes?

When a woman can use her husband's balls as a blanket to cover him while he is sleeping, he should take the clue that it's time for his snip, nip and tuck.

I finally left my office that evening and I was exhausted. Normally I am filled with spit and fire but it was a draining day.

There seemed to be no end to the amount of paperwork sitting on my desk. Where is that Paperwork Reduction Act passed by Congress?

Jumping into my cute little convertible, I headed in whatever direction the wind was blowing. I put on my shades, lowered the top and enjoyed the breeze on me.

Ah, what a feeling it is to be young and alive! I decided I was going to a concert hall that evening. I was smart enough to bring a change of clothing, so after leaving the office, I was all set for my night on the town.

The group playing was a band popular in my teens. The band members in their heyday were already in their thirties. Time had not been kind to them. Instead of appearing in their earlier fifties, they looked as if they were approaching eighty. I am sure drugs had a lot to do with it. The PP - party and price.

A girlfriend of mine was planning to go out with me for the night, but her husband ruined it for us. He is such a jerk! He never wanted to have the children, but they did procreate. So he refuses to stay home with them.

She was able to finally convince him to watch *their* children for the evening. Even though we cleared the date well in advance, he changed his mind at the last minute when his buddies called him for a poker game. It was too late to find a sitter, so she stayed at home and I was left to go alone.

I was in a really bitchy mood, deciding that the stilettos were coming out and some other poor woman like you would get an eye-opening letter.

If I can't save my friend, maybe I could save you, Ashlyn!

The concert was great! I really enjoyed the music but, during the songs that are better left for singing in the shower, I scanned the crowd.

One row in front of my seat, slightly over to my right, was your husband. He had been wearing a t-shirt and, by the looks of it, it had been worn for the last fifteen years. He was a die-hard.

He was drinking and sneaking a drag from his cigarette. The political movement had changed most concert halls from smoking to not smoking. He didn't seem to give a crap. What is a concert without booze and a tobacco high?

I got up from my seat and made my way down the aisle; I walked one row down and turned into his. Squeezing myself through the crowd, I finally reached him.

Acting as if I lost my balance, I fell right on his lap.

At first, his reaction was not a nice one. That was until he realized who fell upon him. I apologized and he forgave me, telling me I could stay there all night if I wanted to. I replied that this seat was much better than mine located in the rafters. Men are gullible.

For the balance of the concert, your husband, his friends and I had a fabulous time! We drank lots of beer, smoked and someone had snuck in those little airplane-type bottles of booze. Rum and coke for everyone!

We we're all disappointed when the concert was over. Looking like a stampede of cattle, everyone tried exiting the building together. Your husband was kind enough to block me from being pushed or shoved by other people.

Our group finally made it to the parking lot. They escorted me to my car. I must have left my trunk slightly ajar because the battery was dead. The boys quickly offered to give me a lift.

Getting in their car was fun! I was sandwiched in the backseat with three of the guys. They were passing me back and forth like some trophy they had won. It reminded me of the childhood song *"Pop Goes the Weasel"*.

During our drive, I found out that all these men had been friends since their college days and it was the same with the wives and you. Kind of neat; all of you married into the same group.

They told me that, once a month, they get out together as a group. They also informed me that they feel as if there are all still in college. Basing my analysis off the way they were acting, I would have to agree. Why bother growing up.

One of the guys in the front seat asked where the car needed to head. The group consensus decided the cool new modern hotel by the bridge. They built an incredible balcony bar on the 20th floor. Off we went.

I was really enjoying myself. All of them had taken great care of themselves. Each worked out daily; they all still retained their own hair. Playing many games of golf gave them beautiful golden tans. They are hotties!

Drinking and dancing then more of the same. The clock swept quickly to closing time. The bartender announced last call and we placed our orders. One of the men left the bar to go to the front desk and get a room. Our party was not over yet!

Taking our glasses with us, we jumped on the elevator and pushed the appropriate floor number. Upon exiting, we located the room that was rented.

It was nothing special; a small room but with a king-size bed. There was five of them and just one of me. Oh, what could we do to pass our time?

Someone went back down to the vehicle to get more alcohol. Funny they had their own bar on wheels.

Refreshing everyone's drinks; I told them that I wanted entertainment. I found the cheap hotel radio and located a station to match my request.

Each man had to perform a strip dance for me. There was a chair in the room at the desk, I pulled it out and positioned it in the middle of the floor, then sat down.

I asked your husband to go first. He started swinging his hips and rocking his pelvis back and forth. He removed his top, took his hands and glided them down to his groin and then around his butt.

He climbed on top of me and made love to me through my clothing. He stood back up, turned around the other way and rode me.

Getting up again, he removed his shoes and socks. Walking around the back of the chair he started kissing my neck and ran his hands down over my swelling chest.

I was really turned on!

He danced back around front, dropped to his knees and separated my legs; he blew his hot breath through my pants. Yes, I could feel it!

He unzipped while rocking to the music and removed his jeans. He was wearing a g-string. I like your husband. Most husbands will not wear butt floss unless we force them during a sexual liaison, and then it's only on for a moment.

He allowed me to touch him; he had hard buns, but that's not the only thing that felt like a rock. He stepped aside and the rest of his buddies, one by one, gave me the show of a lifetime.

After the last one finished and everyone was hot and bothered, we moved to the bed.

Everyone except your husband!

The rest of them all took turns removing my clothing, pouring their drinks on me and licking it off. I had two laying down now and I straddled above them. Bending over the top allowed each man to milk me.

Another one snuck to the head of the bed and balanced on his knees before me. The remaining guy took his position in the rear.

We all worked in unison. It was really an experience. Everyone was having a fantastic time!

Everyone except your husband.

He was just still standing there watching. Ok, maybe that was what he enjoyed doing. But I would at least think he would be choking the monkey. Nope, he just stood there.

The expression on his face was one of desire though; he was sweating and kind of stomping his foot down, as if he had to pee very badly. That was the extent of his participation.

Once I was tired of the other boys, I just had to find out what the deal was with that hubby of yours. I got up from the bed, kick the others off and had him lay down.

I was rubbing myself all over him. I never even had a chance to remove his g-string because he released the dam.

His undies were sticking to him; being considerate I removed them for him.

To my shock, I see your name is tattooed on one side of his love stick. The other side was tattooed "Cheater".

I presume you had embarrassed him enough by now that he no longer cheats on you.

Branding your man, what a great idea!

A Salute to You,
The Other Woman

"Branding"

JOURNAL

Dear Diary,

Tattoos. Body art. I wonder how many women have to look at some guy's body and read another woman's name.

Why do men do that to themselves? Is it a smart chick who gets them drunk and takes them to the local parlor? Does the man just have it done so, when he screwing his girl, he never makes the mistake of calling her by the wrong name?

I have yet to meet a woman with her man's name tattooed on her. I'm sure they're out there but they are quite few in comparison to our population. She may use her children's name but rarely her boyfriend's or husband's. The smarter sex! Why would we do that to ourselves? We know the relationship is not going to last a lifetime, but the mark would.

Men also tattoo the word "Mom" on their bodies. Why? I have often wondered if that's where Mom hits them when they are acting like idiots. Men enjoy target practice; why not give mom the exact area to whack-em. I have never met a girl whose body depicted the word "Dad".

Some men feel the need to tell a story on their torsos. Yep, he is a devil worshipper, likes cartoons, has some Indian blood and a thing for knifes. Opps, almost forgot, Mom beats him and "Betty" was his girlfriend.

I like the idea of penis branding though. In some states adultery is illegal. Inking ownership would make a great punishment for the crime.

I get to sleep in. Thank God it's Friday! Good Night.

Violet

Dear Violet,

I met your husband last night.....

Yippee, it's the weekend! An excuse to sit back and do nothing or do everything which was not accomplished throughout the week.

This beautiful home of mine still requires maintenance and cleaning. I have never been fond of housework; I work for certain luxuries and hiring out all manual labor is one of them. My housekeeper does a terrific job of maintaining my home; it still has the appearance of being brand new. Of course, not having children and a husband helps in that regard.

Visiting friends of mine with a houseful of little creatures, my eyes are always drawn to the stains on the carpeting. Two things pop into my thought process. One: The husband spilled his beer while belching, without a care in the world because he would never clean it up. Two: The potty training of a little one.

One of my dear friends could not get their daughter to use the bathroom for "number two". They tried and tried; hours of waiting and reading stories to the youngster at the commode and still no reward for the parents' effort. The little darling would just find a quiet corner in the house and leave her droppings. The parents had to walk around sniffing the air close to the ground to find her most recent dump site.

I often wondered if her drunken husband was using the child as a scapegoat.

Another dear friend of mine fondly tells a story about her son. Her opinion is, as boys first start walking, they figure out the content of their diaper may contain a weapon of mass destruction or, in some cases, hysteria.

The mother was a mortgage broker. While she was out shopping in town one day, she decided to stroll into the nearest real estate office to say hello. Mortgage people are always trying to drum up additional business; most of them are commission.

Entering the lobby area, she was greeted by a very attractive female realtor. The two of them started chatting when, a few moments later; the real estate agent had this shocked look on her face. My girlfriend followed the angle of the realtor's eyesight to her son. She saw that her two-and-a-half-year old pulled his little wanker out of his dippie and had it on display for the woman.

Embarrassed beyond belief, my friend attempted to tell the realtor she was sorry, all the while she was laughing, snorting and tears were streaming down her face.

The realtor replied "You don't need to apologize; I often have that effect on men."

Amen, how true is that? Of course, blowing wind has the same outcome. Age two; scary isn't it?

So, it's Saturday and the only thing I wanted to do was rest. Playing super hero is a lot of work. My stilettos needed a break.

I had been expecting one visitor. A charity organization was scheduled to come by my home and pick up several boxes of items I was donating.

Do you agree that instead of placing donations in a store to sell, all so some corporate types can collect a paycheck, the items should be loaded into a vacant building for the low income to sift through and take what they want for free? It's sad to profit off the poor. Maybe all the poor families should just move to a third world nation because there they just might receive free aid from the United States.

The doorbell rang and I am sure you can guess who it was. Darn, he was a real handsome chap, I would estimate in his early sixties. I am not normally attracted to older men but this one was very sexy.

He smiled and introduced himself. He continued reading from a clipboard, verifying that he had the right address. Your husband started to recite company policy, which included the need to inspect all items before he could take them.

Opening the door, I requested he follow me to my basement. Reaching the staircase, I motioned for him to go first.

As he was descending the stairs, I watched his backside. Great Butt! I couldn't help but observe it was not saggy or wrinkled. Buns of fun! He must still have an active sex life for his gluts to be so hard. I was very tempted to grab them.

While downstairs, I noticed him checking me out as I pulled some of the boxes in front of us. I could almost feel his eyes undressing me. A split second was all it took for me to decide I should have a little fun with your man.

The first case contained all the lingerie I was giving away. I had begun sorting out my sinful costumes while he adjusted himself. I swear he never noticed doing it.

Stiffening: a verb/action. Cause and effect!

I carefully delivered a statement for him anticipating a particular outcome.

"If my clothing could speak, oh, the secrets they could expose"! I walked towards him holding some of my delectable outfits.

"I am donating them simply because I'm not certain if they look good on me anymore. " I held one up against my firm body.

He quickly grabbed the bait. "If you would like to model them, I would be happy to give you my opinion" adjusting himself once more.

I kissed him on the cheek, grabbed the entire contents of the box and strutted into another room in the basement. He had proceeded to take comfort on one of the sofas. He had to be dumbfounded. I envisioned the following conversation inside his head. "Holy Shit. Thank You God. I can't believe this is happening to me. Oh, wait until I tell the guys! They won't believe me; I will have to keep something as a souvenir. Shit, they still won't believe me. I wish I had my camera."

As an additional compliment to the drama about to unfold, I was softly moaning but loud enough for him to hear me from the other room.

I opened the door and stopped at the frame, pausing for a moment. I had changed into a lacy white teddy with matching panties. A good part of me was still concealed, one reason why I was donating it. The expression on his face was priceless. He could not even speak.

Leaving the immediate area, I strolled in front of him, playing with the hem and twirling my hair.

"What do you think?" I inquired.

His response "I think you look like an Angel and I have died and went to heaven."

I giggled and asked if he wanted to see another one. He answered quickly with another "Yes".

I left him alone and went back to my makeshift changing room. That time I put on a black satin one piece. It rode high on my hipbone and the back was a thong.

Walking out once again, I modeled for him. While turning around to show him the back, I actually heard him gasp.

"That one is really nice too", he said with a voice that was a tad shaky.

I told him I would be right back, grabbing a pair of stilettos in the process of walking away.

Returning to change for the third time, I picked out a red mesh outfit. Made like a dress, it was ankle length but had a slit on the side all the way up to my panties. An additional attribute was that the boob area was cut out. My melons were sticking right through. I headed back out to your husband.

"Wow!", he said as he jumped up from his seating, almost tripping on his tongue.

He asked me for some water. My basement contains a full service bar; retrieving a glass, I filled it with ice water and approached your husband.

As he stood there, it was obvious he was doing his best to not bust the seams off the front of his pants.

He really liked this one. I handed him the glass but not before I dipped my hand inside and removed one of the cubes. Taking the ice, I started circling my melons. The ice had melted against my warm skin and mimicked water flowing from a fountain.
He decided to drink from it. To ensure your husband did not dehydrate, I continued to get more ice, which generated more water for him to quench his thirst.

Boy, what a great time we had been having. Here I thought I was taking it easy that day. This was far more entertaining than I could have imagined.

Getting back to the task at hand, I walked over and retrieved another box; one I have had for a long time. Inside, I found the game "Twister". Do you remember it? Oh, the fun my friends and I use to have as girls. It was meant to prime us for adulthood when those skills of bending like a pretzel would be necessary.

Your husband laughed when he saw it. I inquired if he wanted to play with me and he nodded Yes. Laying out the mat with the colored circles, I spun first.

I placed my one foot on the blue spot. He then took his turn and placed his next to mine on the yellow spot.

Before long, we're very twisted into one another. Your husband soon smartened up and would just stop the spinner on the color he was looking for.

We fell to the ground laughing, but we continued playing.

I ended up on the underneath him. I heard a rip and we both knew the zipper finally gave way. He slid over the slit on my nightie and panties to begin taking my temperature with his built-in thermometer. I guarantee it could have registered as boiling!

We had both worked up a sweat, we were actually sliding on the mat. When he was done playing doctor, he just collapsed on top on me.

Your husband really enjoyed playing games. I am sorry you will never have an opportunity to do that with him anymore. I did send flowers to the funeral home.

In Sympathy,
The Other Woman

"Sex That Kills"
JOURNAL

Dear Diary,

It has been a wild couple of days! This was supposed to be a relaxing weekend but it turned into a nightmare. I only have a few minutes, so I will try and fill in you in a little.

I had to phone the police to let them know there was a dead guy in my house. The first officer who arrived was, of course, the one from the accident I had.

He thought it was funny and said, that maybe we should go get the doc out of jail since he liked dead people. I agreed the doctor did enjoy dead women and as much as I liked "stiff" men, I was not about to ride the one in my basement again.

I pity those wives who find out their husbands had heart attacks while screwing around on them. Two of the most common causes of heart attacks for men: sex and taking a crap.

The officer told me a story about another guy who died on his watch. The woman was so upset because she was separated from her husband, she asked at the autopsy to have his member removed. At least, he died while having sex with his own wife. He had made her extremely happy sexually, so she took his penis to a metals plant and had them pour a bronze mixture on it. He may have died, but his buddy lives forever. His penis remains immortal.

The coroner stopped over to pronounce my charity guy dead. It really wasn't a difficult thing to do; he was blue and not breathing. I had to answer hours of questions from the police. I told them over and over again what had happened. Now, I know this happens with the cops; they want to see if your story has changed, but my opinion is that each officer just wanted to hear the story first hand themselves. All of them made it a point to inform me it was a gun in their pocket. Yeah, right.

I am not a shy person but these servants of the people would not let me change. The outfit was evidence in the crime. A captain said a prosecutor should look at the report. He was not the person to decide if I need to be charged with involuntary manslaughter. Are you kidding me? My Venus Fly Trap is now considered lethal!

Although I am accustomed to being cuffed, they are usually the mink-lined ones. The metal ones are very painful! With my hands behind my back, my breasts sticking right out like headlights, they guided the way to the officer's car.

Later...to the station I must go.

Elisha

Dear Elisha,

I met your husband last night.....

Having a little mishap at home, I was escorted to our local county lockup. I never imaged having to be in such a disgusting environment, but the matter was out of my hands.

Upon entering the devils house, I was immediately transferred to the processing area. It was one large open room, criminals standing in line and police in a firm stance, showing they meant business. Many of the arrested people were so drunk they could barely stand. Some others talked to their invisible friends, while several others had to be subdued.

Wearing close to nothing, I caused quite the stir. My outfit was better suited for one on one entertainment, not an audience. The boys pawed and barked while the girls called me a bitch. The men in uniform grinned.

The officers loved the fact my cha-chas had been sticking right out of my lingerie. Their idea of covering me up consisted of an officer standing there with his hands on my boobs.

All ten had to take turns.

I was the entertainment that evening.

Finally it was my turn to be fingerprinted. They no longer used ink; instead it was a machine that scanned your finger tips.

Once they had the perfect prints, they had me bend over so they could scan the cha-chas, using some lame excuse each chick had different ones and they needed those scans for identification also.

An officer moved me down the line to the camera. Usually they would have taken one front view and one side view. Not these horny cops! They actually had me pose for them.

"Miss, can you please raise your hands above your head holding your hair up?"

"Now, turn around, face the other wall and look over your shoulder back at me."

"Perfect!"

"Can you now please touch your chest?"

"Please turn around once more, bend and grab hold of your toes."

These guys were idiots. However, I had no choice but to obey them.

Moving down the line once more, I was introduced to the search room. I believe a law was passed somewhere, whereby only another woman can search a woman.

Following the legal protocol, they retrieved a female officer to conduct my body-cavity search. The female cop who was already in the room apparently was not trained enough yet to handle this type of search. They fixed their problem easily by getting the really hot redhead from dispatch. It was obvious that the only reason why they switched girls was because the one already in the room was a plain Jane.

They had me spread my legs and place my hands against the wall. Oh, that was gross! How many other hands had been there before?

The hot redhead snapped on her gloves and started to inspect my hair. I felt as if I was in another country where the mothers pick bugs from their children's scalps.

Satisfied that I was not concealing a weapon in my locks, she had me turn my face towards her and open my mouth. I had to stick my tongue out to the left, right, up and down. I did find humor in this exercise.

She proceeded with the body cavity search.

"Do you have anything up there, Miss, that I should be aware of before searching?"

I replied to her "Only a couple thousand stories!"

She gave me a confused expression, so I helped her out.

"No".

A woman's fingers are not as long as a man's. Never having been probed like this by a female, I tried to come in tune with a potential lesbian side. Nope, it just wasn't doing anything for me. It was, however, doing something for the ten male cops watching.

"Rita", one of them said.

"I don't think ya did a thorough enough job."

Rita had to do it again, followed by twelve additional times. Each of the little boys in blue left for a moment, taking turns in the restroom.

After the show and bathroom break was over, I was finally given a green jumper. They thought they were funny because the chest area was cut out of it.

My personal army led me down the hall to open population. One of the lady guards had stepped in the way during transit.

"You can't take her in there like that!" Clearly, she was appalled.

You would have thought I was some horrific criminal because I was escorted by all ten of those officers. We changed direction and headed to a cell. They ignored the words of the female guard.

One of them walked me in and removed the cuffs placed on me after the search. The rest blew me a kiss goodbye and made hand motions against their chests, like they were juggling my breasts or imitation boobies on themselves. Ok, that was immature!

The guard who walked me into the cell just sighed and signaled for the door to be closed after he walked out. Someone had brought a phone for me to use. The famous one phone call!

I dialed my attorney. He was on vacation. Great! The secretary informed me that "Bob the Man is not here but Big Bill is. " I was given to his associate. I explained the circumstances and he said he would come right over.

Not long after, the cell door opened and in walked the guy who was to be my savior-Big Bill. AKA, your husband.

"I spoke with the prosecutor and his office is willing to drop the charges against you." Big Bill was beaming the brightest ray of sunshine.

I couldn't believe this guy was actually happy with himself. There was never a case. They would have to show probable cause. I was not hired by you! I wonder if a scornful wife ever thought about using sex as a way to kill her husband. How could they prove it and what kind of freaky trial would there be? How do you put the other woman on display for the jury as the killer? Would her privates be labeled the assault weapon?

"I will have you out of here in no time" he sat down on my bed still very pleased with himself.

"Why is your jumper missing material?" The lawyer tilted his head sideways.

I replied "Because I was breast feeding the babies out there playing cop dress up".

He chuckled. "I will be right back". Motioning for the cell door to be opened again, he did his best to walk out.

Left in the cell, alone again, I started reading the walls. What else was I going to do just sitting there? Most of the stuff I read was too vulgar for me to repeat to you. Prisoners cannot have writing utensils in the holding tanks; the images on the wall were created with excrement's. Lord, I had to get out of there!

Thankfully, it did not take long for the attorney to return. "Let's blow this joint!" he said.

Not having a car again, I was stuck being driven home by your husband.

He was a little guy: balding, big nose; he might have weighed 115 lbs, a lightweight. I thought, his ego was bigger than him. Most lawyers look like that, don't they? The only thing I found different about him was his walk. He had kind of a limp. Maybe "limp" is not the right word; he had walked as if he had a wooden leg. He could have had some freak accident and this was one of the outcomes.

We made our way very slowly through the parking lot to his car. He helped me in my door and limped- side shuffled over to his. After your husband sat down in the driver's seat, he had to pick up his left leg with both hands and lift it in.

I couldn't imagine having the loss of a limb. Situations like his encourage me to count my blessings.

We arrived at my home about a half hour after we left the station; during the ride our conversation was a bit humorous. He wanted more details of the events which landed me in jail. He expressed that he could see why the old guy stroked out!

Walking in the front door, I offered him something to drink. He informed me usually had his assistant with him when he is on the road. That day though, she was sick. She helps him manage.

I could see why, it would be difficult to carry everything and deal with the leg issue.

Your husband wanted me to know that he felt comfortable with me. Really needing to use the restroom, he inquired if I would mind helping him. Feeling sorry for the guy, I directed him to the closest one and followed him in. As soon as we walked in the bathroom door, he unzipped his pants.

Kindly requesting me to his side, he reached into his pants and started pulling out his hose. I am not shy. I mean, how many of these have I seen in my life?

Wow, he was pretty huge! He had about 6 inches out and continued to keep pulling. 8 inches, 10, 12, Holy crap! Your guy was a giant! At the foot mark, he handed it over to me and braced both hands on the wall before him.

I was standing in the doorway holding his penis. He asked me to walk with it to the toilet and aim. I really felt as if I was playing firewoman and I was putting out a blaze. The stream was so intense I had to spread my feet apart to get better balance. I could understand why he had to brace himself with the wall.

I also had to flush the toilet three times during his urination so it would not overflow!

When some men finish urinating, they can make a sound of relief. This guy did a jungle call. Shaking off the excess was not possible without risking damage to my bathroom.

At his birth, the doctors could have taken the extra skin from his circumcision and donated it to a burn unit for skin grafts. Really, it's that big but you already know that.

Strange things jump into my head all the time; did you know the closest other skin that feels like a man's ball sac is your elbow? Humor me; straighten out your arm and grab the loose skin. I'm right, aren't I?

Well now I had my answer to why he was called Big Bill. I was a little off base with the wooden leg theory, but who would have thought? This is one attorney who really can be labeled a dick!

You don't need to worry about him running around on you honey. Most females are not built like the Grand Canyon; who could handle him?!

Not sure what you do with it,
The Other Woman

"Over Exercised"

JOURNAL

Dear Diary

Wow, what a weird couple of days! I now have a different prospective on the county jail. While I was in my cell, every time one of the female guards walked in front of a cell occupied by a male, the prisoner would hoot and holler. Always being the lucky one, the cell directly across from me had a horn-bug of a guy. He was just whipping it out every chance he could get, after which he would just let it hang out of his jumper for a while.

I noticed that every time he let go of it, it would fall to his right. Every time! This made me only question if it's because men use their right hand so often when they jack off they have loosened the tendons and now their penises naturally falls in that direction. Note: Check next left handed guy to validate if theory is correct.

Finally getting out of there and going home should have been a nice feeling. Instead, I felt as if the circus set up camp in my home. Does God have a sense of humor and that husband was the butt of his joke? It reminded me afterwards of an elephant's trunk. Thank goodness he could not eat with the thing! Imagine the poor wife involved. The only way I could see them doing it was standing up and from the behind. I hope they have a large living area.   Otherwise, this guy could actually be in the next room while screwing his wife. Talk about un-attachment! He could have made a fortune in the porno industry.

I forgot to look at the size of his feet. Darn. Bye!

Autumn

Dear Autumn,

I met your husband last night.....

After a huge day at the office, I decided to pamper myself and went to the local salon and spa. Lord knows I sure did deserve it!

Taking a car is pointless. My salon does not offer valet parking and with it being located in the business district, I would have never found a parking spot.

Waiting for the cab outside my office, my mind drifted to thoughts of my hairdresser. The same man has been doing my hair forever. He's gay and I adore him! He and his flamboyant partner are the perfect match! One plays the more dominant role and it works for them flawlessly. Maybe because they're not married. Anyway...

They have informed me in their life they are only missing one thing. Bitching! The statement causes them to almost roll on the floor in stitches. Struggling to speak through the laughter, they tell me they can live without it. I don't blame them. They never have periods to contend with either.

Periods. a/k/a The Curse. Ok, so here is my opinion of why God would actually do this to females. Back in the beginning of time, women were scarce. This was God's way of giving us a break from all the terrible sexual encounters.

Men had no idea why a woman was bleeding; some may have taken pride in believing they caused it to happen, others could have thought God cursed *them*. It did make the hairy-back naked ape type guys back off for a week.

Why didn't God have the men bleed? At some point, he had to realize what a harsh punishment he bestowed upon us, because after he lets us go through this for 35-40 years, all of a sudden, he grants our wish and the flow stops.

The Almighty was smart with his timing! Leaving us about another thirty years on earth from the last time we bled. The day we walk in those pearly gates, we have forgotten about all the pain and anguish he caused us. His nuts would be spared from being kicked 75 million times and we would not throw him off his cloud for the hell he put us through.

What would be the other purpose of having a menstrual cycle? Oh, yeah, that's right; because our bodies need to think they are pregnant EVERY MONTH and when they realizes they're not, after all the bloating and pain, then we bleed. That's right. Any woman who believes God is female is obviously crazy.

Sorry, back to the story about your husband. I arrived at the salon and over heard one of the nail techs talking about some chick who was just in there. The client had at least twelve layers of polish on her toes. They had to get out the industrial file to chip it away, layer by layer. Yuck. Hello, nail polish remover!

Several office buildings are located to the right of the spa. Looking through the window, I was able to watch people walk to and from one of the office buildings. It does resemble a movie screen. What do all these people do with their lives?

Flashing in front of the window was a delectable man. Yes, your husband. He looked like a movie star. Reading a pizza flyer as he was walking, the essence of him trailed behind his stroll. Everyone that passed him did a double take. Hm, it was going to be a late night at the office for your man. I wondered if he wanted company.

From my angled view out the window, I could see the office building he went into. Judging by the signs out front, it appeared he may be a banker. Financial people are known to be uptight and rigid. I needed to find out if my theory was really true.

My hair was once again a piece of art! I paid my artist, thanked him for his talent and headed out the door on my mission.

Walking a couple of blocks down, I located the pizza joint which was on the flyer. How clever could I be!

Entering through the door, the overwhelming smell of pizza could have knocked you on your butt. The delicious odor had to get into the pores of the workers. When they go home to their counterparts, I could envision the partners being able to engage in sex and have dinner at the same time.

I asked to see the manager.

She was maybe in her mid-twenties. I explained to her that this man walked by me and what an impression he had made. I told her I was not shy and merely wanted to meet him. She said she understood. Being young and single, she knew where I was coming from.

I asked her if he had placed an order giving her the building's address, she scanned the order receipts and, sure enough, he did. It was my lucky day!

Requesting to let me deliver his order, she laughed and said she would play along. The girl disappeared into the back room and reappeared with one of their uniforms.

I paid for the pizza and assured her I would return the shirt to her via *UPS*, if it was ok. She giggled and said it was fine and wished me luck. She obviously had no idea who I was.

Using the restroom, I changed into the shirt. It was an x-large, so it fell more like a dress on me. I removed my shorts and put on the stilettos.

Heading out the door with my pizza in hand, you would not have believed the gawking I was getting on the street. It was funny! Here I was walking with that darn pizza in an oversized shirt and my pumps. Free advertising for the pizza parlor! Companies which have individuals standing outside their business shaking oversized signs are doing it wrong.

The couple of blocks' walk was nothing for me. I have extremely strong legs and my shoes are just an extension of myself; it's as if I am barefoot.

Reaching the office building, I had to push a button and wait for security to buzz me in. Of course they asked who I needed and why I was there. I responded to the secret deep voice that I was delivering a pizza.

I Met Your Husband Last Night

The buzzer rang and I strolled into your husband's office complex. My heels were clicking on the granite floor and echoing throughout the atrium.

I found the elevator and pushed the (Up) symbol. My chariot arrived a few moments later. In case someone was watching the security camera monitors, I flashed the peeking eye while riding up.

Moving gracefully down the hall, I looked left and then right. After passing several doors, I found the right suite number. I was correct in thinking he was a banker, investment banker that is.

I tried the handle but it was locked. Knocking softly, I viewed a silhouette through the glass approaching the door.

Your movie star husband was a little shocked to see *me* as a delivery person. He invited me in and directed me over to a desk a few feet behind him. Making a show of it, I swung my hips in an exaggerated fashion and bent over really far. I mean, really, really far.

He pulled out his wallet from his pocket to pay. I told him the pizza was on me. He replied with "Finally after all of these years of being a devoted customer, I get a freebie!"

Taking what I said seriously, he laid me down on a desk, lifted my uniform shirt, grabbed a slice and placed it on my stomach. He was very talented with his mouth. He was able to takes bites of pizza while barely nipping me with his teeth.

I had always thought it was hard to shock me. Your husband was such a surprise. His only words were for me to put the pizza down and his comment about the Freebie. He never said another thing. His hunger had been immediate!

Maybe I had met my match?

When he was finished with his first slice, he licked his platter clean. I never thought I would enjoy being a plate but your husband changed that for me. Maybe plates are overrated too.

He picked me up into his arms and carried me into another room. Clearing some files from his sofa, he laid me down and continued with his feast.

My shirt was removed, followed by my g-string but leaving the heels on. His talented mouth devoured me whole, lightly sucking and nibbling until he consumed most of me.

He had me kneel on the sofa facing the rear of the couch. He guided his pepperoni stick into my dough and we worked at cooking it. All of a sudden, it seemed he stuffed my crust with his mozzarella cheese.

The only thing I could think of at the time was "God, that was good!"

He fell over to my side on the couch and informed me that he was not expecting the full works. I was not expecting such a rush either.

There was a knock on the door.

He excused his breathless body and left the room. I grabbed my shirt and followed his naked buttocks, avoiding the sweat puddles in the process.

Standing at the doorway was a tall blonde, wearing stilettos of her own. A jumpsuit appeared painted on her, with metal tips at the end of her rockets.

Your husband had this surprised look on his face. He glanced at her, and then back at me, followed by looking at her again.

Apparently your husband had the habit of ordering hookers while claiming to you that he was working late. He just assumed I was his 800-dial a girl.

Next Time I Order Pizza, I will think about you,
The Other Woman

"Paying For Pleasure"

JOURNAL

Dear Diary,

I often wonder why men would order prostitutes. Is it because they are living out a fantasy or because their wives are not giving them any at home? Could it be just shear boredom or do they like playing Russian roulette with disease?

Is it like ordering pizza when men call one of those services?

"Yes, I am looking for a blonde with big hooters, long legs which are tan, the ability to swallow and recently tested for STD's. Please make sure she can spin like a top when I have her suspended from the ceiling fan."

What happens to these women later in life when hooking was their only trade? When they lose their teeth after old age and lack of dental care, do they then market themselves as the "Gum Yum Queens"? Customers are guaranteed to not experience pain.

That reminds me of something else. As protective as men are about their buddies, they sure place enough trust in girls to not just bite it off!

How many hookers are there? More than you would think! They can be found in every city across the nation. Many guys will just leave town as to not get caught by their wives. Walk into any hotel bar in Vegas, the girl sitting by herself is a hooker. You have to look quick though, because someone's husband will grab her up fast. Don't worry, another one will just sit right down.

Sienna

Dear Sienna,

I met your husband last night.....

I was recently speaking to a friend of mine about feminine deodorant spray. Who was it that invented it? What are they trying to tell us?

When should this spray be used? It has been marketed to use anytime for a quick freshen-up. If someone needs to use spray, the girl is not showering, and she should be.

I have never found myself running into the bathroom and grabbing a can from my purse, pulling down my undies and spraying a bit before a man decides to visit.

The natural odor of a woman is what attracts a man. The scent of a woman! Which is also why dogs sniff the back end of other dogs, he is just trying to find the female. If it has become pungent, then cleansing is in order.

As far as "that time of the month", there is nothing you can do. A spray would not deplete the odor; it would only mix with it. It would be as if a fish were wearing perfume. Not a pleasant thought.

We can't help the smell of old blood from that time of the month. It's tissue which has died. I have never smelled a cadaver; maybe it's close. Just another reason why tampons are so much better than pads; gotta keep the odor in, not out. Of course, by using something we love so much, we can die from toxic shock syndrome. Due to the popularity of the product, we seem to choose death over discomfort and odor.

It was that time of the month for me. Yes, even I am subjected to the laws of Mother Nature. I swear - what a pain in the ass it is! However, always up for a good time, I grabbed the stilettos and headed out for the evening. My bag stuffed with little white mice.

I live close to a very popular park. People bring their families there during the day, but at night it becomes a concert park.

Blankets and coolers cover the grounds. The stage is filled with musicians and their equipment.

I had no idea what group was giving the night's performance; it really did not matter much. It was the ambiance I was looking forward to.

Over to my right under a large tree, I found your husband. He was a handsome guy, wearing an athletic-type outfit and strumming a guitar. The tree provided cover from the sun and support for his back.

Gracefully making my way over to him, I tucked my skirt under my backside and sat down on his blanket. So as not to interrupt the beautiful sounds streaming from his guitar, I did not speak.

After approximately a half-hour of listening and feeling the melody, I was able to lay back and relax further. The concert was not expected to start until it was dark. Girls can become so transfixed on musicians; we easily fall in love. These artists remind me of snake charmers. A spell is placed on us and the groupie is born.

I noticed his fingers and how they moved in such harmony as he was picking at the strings. Strong fingers! He was humming a song but he was so quiet I could not hear the words. Closing my eyes, I could see the notes swirling around us.

Your husband appeared to be pretty happy with my company. Every once in a while, he would look to see if I was still interested in the mood he was setting for me. Possibly, he was checking to see if he conjured enough of a spell yet to render me helpless.

He finally laid down his guitar, opened up a cooler he had with him and handed me a miniature bottle of wine.

He had started spinning his wedding ring on his finger. Have you ever noticed married people doing that; either they hide it or unconsciously they play with it? I asked him where you were; he replied that you were at home with the kids. He continued by informing me that the two of you actually had met right there at the park. Even after all of these years, he still went to be one with nature but always thought about you.

Your husband also spoke of enjoying the birds and people watching.   Every once in a while, someone thought he was homeless and they would toss coins on his blanket. When leaving the park, he would deposit the token gestures in the fountain.

Always inquisitive, I had to ask him if he was happy in his relationship. He paused for a moment and told me that for the most part, "Yes" he was. But things did change over the years. It seemed your love life was like a TV rerun, nothing new; the same hum-drum. In the beginning, all you had to do was walk by and "wham", he was aroused. Now, you actually have to work on it, molding the clay over and over again before it would become a larger object. The goal was to make something which could work.

I thought to myself, maybe he was a perfect candidate for erectile dysfunction medication. It's much easier to blame the wife, is it not? "Dude, you have strangled your little friend so many times over the years, the blood vessels are constricted, and the blood cannot pump through anymore. You over played with your toy and now its broke". I wanted to inform him of my theory. Instead, I acted as if sympathy was running through my veins.

I agreed with him. Sometimes, being with the same person to long, relationships can lose their spark. Couples misplace their interest in relighting the candle which once burned so hot. Those couples have children and become parents, only to turn into their own parents. It also does not help when these parents have their children sleep with them. Did you do that?

I love sex, so when I hear these things coming from men or women, it really bothers me. He also reported that every time you two do have sex, it is his idea and you seem to be repulsed by even getting close to him. I do have a flaw; I am overly opinionated when it comes to love. If you are nauseated and that your skin crawls when he touches you, maybe you should consider the relationship is over. You can either get really drunk every night or file for divorce.

I gave him some ideas to work on with you. Not that it may help your situation. Throughout all this conversation, we continued drinking more wine. We were both really buzzed when the concert finally started.

It was strictly music, no vocals. The sound was amazing and the stars in the sky added to the tone. The air become chilly; your considerate husband noticed I was cold and snuggled right up to me. It was so sweet. I looked up at him to thank him for his warmth and he planted a warm seductive kiss on me. What is a girl to do?

Well, this girl took advantage of the atmosphere and responded in a manner he was happy with.

We were only laying on part of the blanket, so he was able to use the other half to cover us. I felt like a mummy; we were wrapped so tightly together.

Noting this guy has not had a good pump out of his tank for awhile, I snuck my hand under the cover. At first I was messing around on the outside of his jeans, stroking him and tilting my lips up for continued kisses.

While I was giving him mouth to mouth, I unzipped his pants and pulled out the bear. He was warm and very stiff. No molding required here. Of course, it had been hibernating for awhile.

The concert was ending but there was a fireworks display afterward. I took advantage of the diversion and slid my head under the covers to meet the grizzly live. All of a sudden, I was overwhelmed with the odor of armpits on fire.

Jumping up from the blanket, I bent over to the side and threw up. Now I know why you are repulsed. Have you never said anything to him?

Enclosing Nose Plugs,
The Other Woman

"Sweat Is Not Sweet"

JOURNAL

Dear Diary,

This beautiful evening I had was ruined by human pollution.

I so felt bad for him. His wife acted revolted whenever he approached her for sex. I can see why! The sweat glands by his ball sac released such a terrible odor!

Going back to those manufactures distributing feminine deodorizers, why on earth have they not made "The Men's Ball Spray"?

Would it be too embarrassing for a male to purchase it? I think these gentlemen sitting at their corporate marketing brainstorming sessions have forgotten the fact many women will buy it for their men!

Companies make deodorizer for everything else. We have foot spray, mouth wash, and scented pads - but where is the ball spray?

Those are some major glands down there. Clothing keeps them trapped! Our guys sweat! There is no circulation. It's not their fault; they are made that way. But God never thought humans were going to be wearing clothing.

And men wonder why their girls are not sucking the straw anymore.

How many times have you seen a man lift their arms and smell their pits? They are not flexible enough to smell their crotches. Probably a good thing!   Anyway, they have no idea they are funktified, unless we tell them.

Maybe I should run for Attorney General, I would make major changes in social acceptance and behavior. I would also contract an engineer to develop a venting system in men's clothing.

Good Night.

<u>Mary Anne</u>

Dear Mary Anne,

I met your husband last night…..

How many R-rated movies have you watched where you went to the theater and they flash a woman naked flesh? Would it be safe to say 85%? I think I am being kind with that number.

They never show the man! Every once in an eclipse year they might give us a film which shows a partial butt shot, but usually that's the extent of it. Are we supposed to be happy with that?

The movie industry is defiantly run by men! They don't want us to see the graphic images of other males. As second class citizens, female enjoyment is not considered.

I was in the sex toy shop, passing by some of the x-rated movies and I thought "This is about the only time we can see it all!" A shame, really!

It's not as if they are all the same. Penises come in different colors, shapes and sizes. Some have great personalities and will greet you upon introduction. Others are on the shy side. Some are healthy and some are sick.

Men love the peep booths at these types of stores! Ugh. Guys walk in the back and take a seat. Insert money into a machine and Presto! a curtain opens. They remove their wankers and, while the woman is masturbating for the 100th time that day, these men join in and spray the booth. Who has the job of cleaning up the mess? Yuck! Maybe the jack-off box never does get cleaned.

Most women will not come into a store like the one I am speaking about. I gather they are embarrassed. Lord knows, they are not taking a trip to the peep booth, but the store itself can be a fun experience. If a girl is purchasing a gag gift for a friend, she might go but even then a friend or two will be in tow.

Acting silly as they go down the aisle, comments like "Oh my God, what do you do with that?", "Hum, that looks like fun!"and "Why do we need men?" escape their mouths. Some girls secretly wishing they could buy many of the toys they see, but what would their friends think?

Mail order and on-line purchasing have made it a little easier for ladies, but then they consider the look on the postal worker's face when the box arrives.

Women think too much.

A friend of mine is not overly shy; she won't purchase toys at the store but she will do mail order. I was at her home, house sitting. She and her husband happened to be out of town and someone needed to tend to their dog.

It was a beautiful day as I was lounging out at the pool, a cocktail in one hand and one of those erotic romance novels in my other. Men sport smutty magazines, the internet, strip clubs and cable. Women purchase trashy books. When I am at a store and a woman purchases one, I am so tempted to say. "Yep, you're going to have fun tonight! Skip right to chapter three, page 53." Women just handle masturbation with more class.

The yard is a built-in paradise. The pool is Olympic size with second and third-tier waterfalls. The sound of running water makes an extremely relaxing environment. Never wanting tan lines, sunbathing nude was my only option.

I found myself enjoying the hot rays from the sun and the steamy love scenes in the book. Authors really should put in just a couple more in each novel.

My friends were expected home at anytime on that day. I have been so busy at work, that particular day was the first time since they've been gone to which I had a chance to enjoy their oasis.

Right smack dab in the middle of the characters getting it on, the doorbell rang.

I walked to the front of the house and I could see the mailman through the entry door. Your husband looked really cute in his little shorts. His mouth hung open as I approached. I was still naked.

As I opened the door, he said he had a package for special delivery. It was a larger box and a little bulky. It was one of those packages which are difficult to hold but your man miraculously had grown a shelf out of his pants, so he was able to let it rest there.

I have always been one those girls attracted to men in uniform. He did not look as if he just left a fleet from sea; he looked more like a *Boy Scout*. Can't have it all; close enough, I thought.

I asked him to come in. He followed me to the nearest table and put the package down. I, of course, had to address the bulge.

"You must be very happy to see me!" He replied. "You have no idea! Viewing goddesses like you is one of the perks of my job." He continued, "However, due to all of the new construction homes, most mailboxes are now on the road. My peeks inside homes are now very limited, unless, of course, I have to take a package to the door. Besides delivering mail in this neighborhood, I also live around here. Honestly speaking, I would never want to see most of the housewives around here naked! I like cottage cheese in my salad, not on my women".

Your husband is an asshole!

I gave him my charming smile "I am pleased to make your day. It is pretty hot out there; would you like something to drink?" He nodded his yes. I went to the refrigerator and pulled out bottled water and handed it to him. "Thank you" he replied and then continued "I am sorry if I am staring at you, but I can't help but admire your beauty."

I walked back over to the box on the table to see what my friends had delivered. The return label was stamped with "More Lov'in Inc.". Curiosity overcame me; I just had to open the box.

I started peeling back the tape, opened the flaps and brushed aside the foam peanuts. To my delight I found a DVD titled "How to Beg for More". It appeared to be a step-by-step instructional video. Also in the box I found a man's outfit, tie straps, a mask and, of course, a whip. Everything was made in leather. My favorite!

"Wow!" your husband expressed his excitement. I asked him if you participated in anything like this and he said "No", you refused to explore other avenues of sexual gratification.

I asked him if he wanted to play. He immediately answered with "Yes".

Taking him to the bedroom, I had him remove all his clothing and put on the outfit from the box. He looked really Wild! The pants had each of the butt cheeks cut out, the leather wrapped around the front and there was only a hole for his extension of himself to poke through. The leather continued up his chest and around his neck. Silver spiky prongs laced him like a dog collar.

I opened up the cabinet containing the television; it was in a perfect position before the bed. I requested he lay down on his stomach with his head towards the TV and his feet touching the headboard.

Popping in the DVD, the instructions with video images had begun playing on the screen.

Your husband had really enjoyed all of the spanking and whipping. The instructions on the screen were very easy to follow.

He even barked on cue. Maybe men can be trained after all.

The straps were even more fun. Making him flip back over with his back against the mattress, I tied his arms and legs to the four corners of the bed.

I was going down on him and, finally, after all of the torture your man went through, I thought he couldn't take it anymore and he screamed.

"Jesus Christ! Oh Mary, Mother Of God!"

Now, I had been complimented before on my skills but rarely do I get placed in that category. I heard a sound behind me.

I then discovered your Adam did not release his seed, I spun around to find you standing there.

Sorry Mary!
The Other Woman

"Treat Him Like The Dog He Is"

JOURNAL

Dear Diary,

Just another interesting day in my life!

I would never want the wife to catch her husband actually in the act. With them living in the same neighborhood as his route, she drove past his mail truck when she went grocery shopping. On her way back from the store, an hour later, she noticed his truck still in the same parked position.

She was ringing the bell and knocking, but we could not hear her over the DVD playing and her husband's moans.

An additional surprise was that she ended up joining us. Who would have thought? I still found it necessary to send an apology.

She asked for the whip and started to beat the crap out of him. I believe she was really enjoying herself. She was biting down really hard on her teeth; it appeared she was in as much pain as he was.

I heard him mumble "Mommy" once or twice through the gag she placed on him. That only had her start screaming "That's right, who's your Mommy now!!?"

She found the dog's leash and attached it to him and proceeded to walk him outside. She had him on all fours whipping his butt and pulling hard on the choke chain. He was submissive and obedient!

Off they went. What sucks is they took my friends' outfit with them. Now I owe my friend a kinky outfit and a dog leash.

Oh well. Good Night!

Gabriela

Dear Gabriela,

I met your husband last night.....

What is with the lack of manners in a great portion of married men? I really love being single! The men will actually open a car door for me. Pull out my seat at dinner. Take my hand and equally walk with me instead of twelve paces ahead.

When you're married, all of that changes. They race out to the car, forget about you and, if you don't make it in time before he cranks the engine, he just may leave without you! Never even noticing you never got in the car.

Dinner. Gross! It some countries, it is a compliment to belch after a good meal. But not here in the good old USA! It's vulgar and disgusting. They reach down really low to the pit of their being and release their burp. Sometimes it's so powerful; it blows the girl's hair back. Then they end it with, "Auhhh" while rubbing the basketball they swallowed at some point in their life.

Walking. The perfect sign to see if a couple is married from a distance. Men try blaming it on the fact their legs are longer. The real reason is because they don't want anyone else to know the other person is their wife.

Bathroom visits. Many wives have told me of their husbands grunting very loud from the bathroom, it sounds as if they are giving birth. Some males are so proud of the birthing experience they want to share the joy of what they delivered with their girl.

"Hey Honey, come look at this! It's a three-flusher!" or thrilled they have made some kind of art; "Babe! It fell in a coil and looks like a big snake, come here!" After years of marriage, they begin to leave the door open, which allows them to share the experience easier. If they are blessed, men are able to tuck their friend inside the toilet; if not, I would never recommend that the wife purchase a black light, because, through their grunts in delivery, they may pass urine and wifey would be horrified to see what's really on her walls.

This is the one which gets me the most. The releasing of toxic human substance into our air supply. You may know this as farting. The dictionary has the following definition: to expel a flatus through the anus. Never in my life have I ever heard of "Flatus", so here is the definition: intestinal gas produced by bacterial action on waste matter in our intestines. I always thought the word "Fart" was slang but, after research, I see I was mistaken. It really is in the dictionary. Of course, *Webster* is a guy so why not list something which men are proud of.

Married men release their flatus just about any time. I was told once by a man they love their own flavor/brand. As the wife is turning green, the husband is inhaling deeply with a smile. It could add to the problem. You see, the odor is so bad anyway; now the men inhale deeply, recycling their flatuses. The smell just gets worse each time. Like a wine that ages, so do men's flatuses.

Oh, how about those really sick pigs that pull their wife under the blanket and release gas. It's only my opinion but I think they are trying to kill their wives. When a woman dies young and they cannot find a cause during autopsy, the coroner never bothers to check for flatus overdose. I think they should!

I Met Your Husband Last Night

I never have to deal with any of that. Men can behave humanly while trying to impress a girl. See, that's the key - if your man does any of the above, he's not trying to impress you anymore or, to put it bluntly, he does not care what you think. Truth hurts sometimes, I know.

Anyway, about your husband! He sure was a firecracker!

A friend of mine was having a cocktail party for business associates. Her home was quite large; it was easily able to fit the hundred people in attendance.

I have always had an eagle eye, the ability to locate the hottest man in record time. This trait of mine tracks them like radar.

Your husband was very quickly on my scope. I could hear the blip in my head getting louder as I approached him. I am certain it was my pulse rate raging through me the closer I entered into his space.

The hostess had hired servers to walk within the crowd and serve cocktails and appetizers. One of the wait staff was approaching your husband as I was. He was carrying chilled shrimp with the tails already removed.

As your man was viewing the delicious spread on the platter, I walked up, snatched one of the shrimp and put it into his mouth. He not only took the shrimp with his luscious lips, he latched onto my hand, held it in place and absorbed my finger also.

"Thank you. And now you are all clean" he had said with a devilish grin. After a little introduction, he took me out on the balcony.

Playing a little dumb for theatrics, I queried about you. He replied you were at home and that he had been out of town. He never thought he was going to be back in enough time to make the gathering we were at. His travel was cut short and the party was on his way home, so he stopped by. I am so very pleased he did.

His phone rang. Your husband excused himself, but never left my side. After a few minutes or so, the call ended. He said you had decided to go see a movie and then cocktails afterward with a friend of yours and, because you did not want to drink and drive, you were staying at your friend's house. Your tasty-looking gent also said you had no idea he was already back in town and you wanted to let him know what you were doing in case he called and did not get an answer on your phone.

Very sweet. I was surprised that after all of these years of marriage, you were still considerate. Heck, if I had a husband and he was out of town, I do not believe I would bother calling him. He did not bother telling you he was back, did he?

We strolled arm in arm back to the party and socialized with more people when he whispered in my ear "Let's get out of here". His warm breath sent chills down my spine. Of course I had to agree with him.

I left my car and had ridden with your really spicy boy. During the first part of the car ride, I was eating him with my eyes.

It must be interesting to be married to an astronaut. Have you ever had sex with him in the zero gravity space training room? I can't help but think how wild it would be! If the pounding is intense, would the two of you resemble a game of *Pong*? Are those rooms padded?

We had been chit-chatting about his work during the drive. He told me that sometimes he is gone for months at a time, hanging out there in space with the aliens. He was living his childhood dream.

Your husband had an extremely seductive voice. I was drawn to him. He continued to tell me tales and, at some time during our lovely ride, I placed my hand on his leg.

I was rubbing up and down his thigh; I would then cut across his stomach and slide my hand down his other leg, never touching the space monkey! I curled up really close to him, kissed down the length of his neck and traced his ear with my eager tongue, lightly blowing my hot breath down each path I had taken. I am getting excited again just writing this letter to you.

Through pleasure of touch, I finally had moved my hand to his center gravity. Let me tell you - there was no space left in there. Massaging his oxygen hose, I was having a hard time breathing, leaving myself with no choice but to take oxygen for myself.

At the time, he was still trying to drive without crashing. I had heard a large truck zoom by, hooking his horn. Trucker language for "Damn, are you lucky, Dude!"

Your husband told me he had never cheated on you and never planned to in the future. Ok, how silly was that statement when I was still getting breathing treatments from his lap. He gave me some lame presidential excuse which included "oral sex does not constitute sexual relations".

He hushed for a moment to enjoy the drive when I almost choked on the increased air flow from his hose. He repeated out loud to me while laughing "I have never had sexual intercourse with that woman!". He spoke the statement with a southern drawl. My breathing treatment was over.

I sat up again and reapplied my lip gloss. Looking out the window, I inquired about our current location. He pointed to a large home down the street we had been traveling and said: "That's my house." I was shocked and asked him about you; I was reminded you were gone for the evening.

Pulling into the driveway, a family of deer was trotting through your yard. It was so pretty! In the city, I never see anything like that. The closest thing which came to mind would be a group of rats scurrying across a littered street.

He opened your front door, carried me over the threshold, walked me to a sofa, put me down and planted a passionate kiss on me.

We heard a noise; he seemed rather startled and suddenly, out of nowhere, your dog came running out and tackled your husband. Letting your puppy outside, he reached for my hand and led me to your bedroom.

Gently lifting me to your bed while kissing my neck, he climbed on and joined me. Lifting my dress up, he continued kisses on the inside of my thighs. Mr. Astronaut would barely brush over the space that connects my two legs with his hot breathing. Lounging his tongue finally into my pudding, he lapped it up like the sweet treat is was. I was in heaven!

Your dog was making all sorts of noises, ruining some of my concentration and pleasure. Finally, I interrupted your space guy and asked him to get the dog out of the room. I left my legs just as they were positioned; I wouldn't want him to think the store was closed.

He turned around and had begun to walk out of the room towards the back door, but stopped suddenly. He paused briefly, glanced over to me; then walked to the closet, followed by another look at me.

He opened the jarred closet door, I had propped myself on my elbows for a better look and he found you.

Your husband and I were extremely surprised to find you in there, but more amazing was your position. You almost looked like the dog because you were on all fours; your tail resembled a man. Hm, it was a man. How on earth did he get himself stuck to your back end? I guess the entire ruckus was from the two of you.

Your husband was very shocked, let me tell you. His best friend in the closet with you said; "Well, you caught us with our pants down!"

What a strange situation. As your husband is screaming at you about cheating and telling you he has never cheated, I was laughing my butt off.

I called a cab and your lover decided to join me. Come on, I still had pudding left in the bowl; I certainly wasn't going to let it go to waste!

Your lover told me that you had no idea your husband and I came home. It was his idea for the two of you to get in the closet; he was just being careful. But then he noticed your husband and me in the bedroom and decided he was able to watch the show on your bed and bang you at the same time. You really should pay more attention; maybe if you would have, you could have kept your mouth shut and would never have been caught. Your night was full of surprises, wasn't it?

Still Waiting For the Cigar,
The Other Woman

"Marriage Licenses Should Expire"

JOURNAL

Dear Diary,

I have heard too many times over the years that men do not think having oral sex is committing adultery.

"Eat'in ain't cheat in' " It is, in my opinion, cheating! No ifs, ands or buts about it.

This was a smart lady though; she did not swallow completely that her husband was faithful, so during his trips, she just banged his best friend.

I rarely come across a lady which comes to her senses and decides to have a little fun of her own.

One sad part is that hubby was so mad, he will file for divorce. Never mind the fact he was with me, in *their* bedroom. Stupid man, but she was one smart woman!

As I walked out their door, I could hear her screaming and calling her husband a pig, she was tired of him polluting the house and her.

They were married too long I think. Maybe marriage licenses should expire! Most everything else does; drivers licenses, fishing, hunting, nursing, real estate, doctors, lawyers, etc. We only have legal liability of kids until age eighteen!

Licenses expire to ensure that if the person holding the license had changed, lost their mind or just are not interested anymore, they are required to reapply and qualify again. All known parties must agree.

Think of all of the marriages which could be saved by knowing the other person could walk away so easily. People would try harder. Those licenses which can't be salvaged would make divorce court obsolete. Expiration date = you are single!

Everyone should write their Representative/Senator. We could call it the "Marriage License Expiration to defeat The Other Woman Bill" or maybe it's the "I May Grow to Hate Him/Her Bill".

I'm trying my hand at golf tomorrow. Or should I say, I'll watch golf tomorrow from the clubhouse!

Good Night!

<u>Bubbles</u>

Dear Bubbles,

I met your husband last night.....

I have met him many times before, of course. The three of us have been friends for a very long time.

I treasure our friendship, Bubbles. You have always been there for me, and there are no words which measure up with how grateful I am to know you. You are my very best friend.

It is amazing to me how good the years have been to you; you become more beautiful with every passing year. You have such a sex-kitten way about you. I love our inside joke that you are "Man's Best Friend" because of the reactions on their faces when you brush by or how they flock to you when we are out. Just like *Batman and Robin*, you are my super hero sidekick.

God graced you with such a hot body! Tiny and curvy plus your natural big boobs give you that *Playboy Bunny* look. Your husband is one lucky man. I have told you a thousand times and I think I have told him two thousand times!

Because we are friends, we share all of our stories with each other. Since I am the single one, my stories seem to be much more exciting than yours. Never meaning to offend you; but your sex life is kind of boring. But you already knew that.

I appreciate the fact you finally were fed up enough that you expanded your toy collection. Of course, I have dabbled with my share of tools but I was so surprised to hear some of the latest products available.

We have often said that receiving oral sex is a mandatory requirement for both of us. I remember you often complaining your husband just does not travel south anymore. I know for a fact that you have supplied him with a compass. Could that be why so many women sneak off and have women lovers? Men and women are trained at birth to suckle....how do these men misplace that instinct?

I loved hearing about your new toy....a machine you can sit on and rediscover what you have been missing. How cool is that? I find irresistible the fact you can just plug it in the wall instead of having to worry about batteries. Lord knows, you would have spent a fortune at the drugstore. So instead of looking elsewhere, you improvised. Not quite the same thing as a moustache ride, but that's his loss now.

I take pleasure in paying close attention to you and hearing of the things which bother you. The opportunity to help you with any of your bedroom concerns never really presented itself before, until last night.

There was a golf outing at the country club. Being a social member, I like to visit and have cocktails. Your husband was sitting with a bunch of his buddies, and they were smashed.

Christmas was only a couple days away, and one of the gag gifts that seemed to be circulating was the "Chia Pet." The boys had evidently chipped in and bought one for their favorite waitress. You and I know she would have preferred the cash. When I first saw it, I laughed too, but there was something else about it that was triggering a thought in my mind. It was on the tip of my tongue...gag gift....*Chia Pet*...gag....*Chia*. I remembered! I know what I am getting you for Christmas!

I am writing this to you as if it was happening now; I want you to be a part of this experience.

Now for the tough part. "Excuse me, waitress?" "Another drink?" Silly question. "Yes, please, and can I also have a fifth of the house vodka and an empty shot glass?" She nods and strolls away as I dig into my purse for a shiny quarter.

To your husband and his friends I announce, "Quarter bounce time!" They laughed; how many years since we played that? I never lost a single game in college. These guys didn't stand a chance.

I won, and they not only lost, but they were all in vodka fogs. I put your husband's arm around my neck, and led him to the car. I drove us back to my house, opened the door, and deposited him on my kitchen floor. Then I skipped into the bathroom and found my kit. You are going to be so happy with me! The gag gift reminded me of one of your enduring requests, one he would never do; shave his pubes!

I remember you saying you would be happy with a trim job. Not that he wasn't clean; it was just about looking tidier down there.

You and I would laugh until we cried about being cat-like with the hairballs our men produced and the ones they were kind enough to deposit into our mouths.

I even told him once he needed to do it for you, and I believe his direct quote was some caveman reference to "pushin' and cushin' ".

He is passed out cold! I unzip him and slide down his pants. Hey, nicely endowed! I could now see what you had been talking about, the forest was so thick, and it was difficult to find the tree stump.

The small scissors I had was not enough to handle the beginning stages of this job. I had to get those orange commercial type of scissors out of the junk drawer in the kitchen.

Finally there was enough trimming done that I could switch over to the smaller shears.

I glanced to the side of your passed-out husband and notice the cat. Wait, I don't have a cat. Thirty five years of no trimming and the discarding was so large, it resembled a curled up feline. You poor girl!

He always said, "Trimming down there is not a manly thing. What would the guys in the locker room think if I shaved like that?" He will soon know, girlfriend.

When I was down to seeing skin, I switched to a razor. He might be happy about one thing. He is big, and will look even bigger now!

I continued shaving and left my initials. This way when he woke up from his drunken stupor, he would know it was I that did this to him. I figured you would find the humor in that.

I Met Your Husband Last Night

How much do you want to bet he picks up the razor himself to remove my mark? Other than the small area of fuzz, he is bald as an eagle, baby!

I sent him home in a cab with note pinned to his shirt, which said, "Merry Christmas! Enjoy your anti-*Chia Pet*!"

Love ya girl!
The Other Woman

"Being Tidy"

JOURNAL

Dear Diary,

That was too much fun! The joy in giving! I don't believe I could have bought a better present at the store for my buddy.

Her husband will be mad at me for a while but it will grow back (hopefully she won't let it) and he will get over it.

Shaving: it's such a necessary thing to do. Ok, maybe God did not intend us to shave. His intention was to keep us warm. Human fur, I suppose, but God never realized we would have global warming.

It's hot as hell in the summer! Deodorant for those who wear it, is a life saver to the rest of the population.

I have been trapped in too many crowds where you could smell the person who does not use it and I want to puke. God installed a built in "Notify-er" in each of us. If you smell... bathe. I assume some individuals "Notify-er" just does not work.

Where are the science experiments on finding the "Notify-er" in the human body and correcting it with out-patient surgery? Medicaid could cover the costs for those who can't afford it. No wonder government workers are so cranky; they have to smell people all day.

Another thing I could never understand is why everyone is so polite about human pollution. Nobody ever says anything to the smelly person. Why is that? Maybe the smell-yuns don't know. Someone should tell them.

I decided to finally start carrying those one-dollar drugstore mini antiperspirants in my purse with me. When my smell detector begins buzzing, I walk right up to the person and, in a clear voice, so there is no confusion, I enlighten them. "Hey, you smell really bad. Seriously, you stink! Take this and use it." Then I walk away.

Just doing my part for the people.

Tomorrow is a day of extra income. Sometimes I make extra money on the side, it gives me something to do and occasionally it sends me further on my mission.

Sleepy girl signing off,
Good Night.

Hallie

Dear Hallie,

I met your husband last night.....

The Bachelor party; the final night as a free person! What do they do with it? Bachelor parties can either be simple or extreme. It will always depend on what kind of friends the future husband has.

Is the best man single himself and thinks his buddy is crazy for getting married? Or is he old and married and will put together an evening more on the mellow side?

How much alcohol will they pour down the groom's throat? The rest of the boys have come out to play for the celebration may also be an occasion to sow some wild oats.

An evening of booze and sex? Perhaps.

Your sweetheart was in attendance last night. I will start at the beginning of the story for you.

I have a chauffeur's license and, on occasion, either to make extra money or just for the fun of it, I will drive people in a beautiful black stretch limousine. They name the destination and I deliver.

I received a phone call a few weeks back from a mutual friend of the groom. He knew about my license and asked if I would drive the wild men out for a night of playing and hunting. It was a bachelor party, how could I resist?

I picked up about 16 guys, one of them was your husband, and all of them were very cute!

My uniform consisted of a black leather bra with a matching black mini skirt, fishnet stockings and the final touch of my stilettos. My long hair was flowing down my back and my nails painted lipstick red to match my shoes. I was dripping with sex appeal. The guys seemed very excited to have me as a driver.

In the back of the car, the boys were pouring drinks, laughing and having a great time. They left the divider down so they could have me join in the fun. Their first destination was to the local watering hole.

The building looked as if it was falling down. The craters in the parking lot could have swallowed the cars in full and the clientele already inside was from the *Twilight Zone*.

Many of the current customers had never heard of dental care; they were able to eat their greasy bar food without even opening their upper and lower jaws. The food slides right in the gaps, where once were teeth.

The bar only served beverages in cans. No glass allowed there; too many bar fights. To make you feel a little better, there was no way your husband was going to mess with any of these ladies, regardless of how much alcohol he consumed.

The groom was on his way to getting plastered. Someone brought in a beer bong and the boys just kept pouring beer into the funnel. Instant buzz!

They finally decided to move on from that experience; we jumped back into the safety of the limo.

Next stop was the topless joint.

The first thing you notice when walking in are the showers. Yes, real showers made for about four people each, all glass. That way everyone in the bar can watch.

Your husband was in heaven! The boys retrieved the groom; paid the hefty price, stripped him down and had him walk into the wash cube.

Two completely naked ladies waited for him. He was sandwiched between them as they rubbed their skin against his. The groom did keep his undies on but as a tribute to them both, he had raised his flagpole.

While the groom was getting clean, the rest of the boys were in the several hot tubs surrounding the dance stage. Yes, your husband was having a ball. Dancers kept jumping in and out of the tub with him.

The groom had his hands up against one of the glass walls; the two girls had soaped him down. He was one giant bubble. His flagpole slipped a little and, instead of sticking straight out, it was straight up and peeking over the top of his underwear.

Being the kind girls they were, they washed that body part too. The act just encouraged the groom to lose the underwear.

Your husband asked me to join him in the tub but management stopped me because I would be taking attention away from the dancers. All I could do was sit there and watch.

Three ladies had your man cornered in the tub, asking me to grab more money for him out of his wallet. I handed each girl a twenty-dollar bill. One was Asian, one was Spanish and one was African-American. Each of them very striking!

After closing the bar, our passenger count in the limo grew by another three. I am sure you figured out how that came to be. They asked me to drive to your house; you happened to be away visiting family with the kids.

Before long, we pulled in your driveway and the party was now in your living room. Someone turned on the music and the girls started dancing with each other. The ritual at first was pleasant and then it turned into an animalistic dance. The girls were pawing at each other and the guys were cheering them on. The lesbian acts sent many of the guys over the edge. Testosterone could have blown the roof off of the house.

At a break in a song, the girls left the room in search of your bedroom. A few moments later they returned, wearing clothing once again. Your husband had a look of recognition. Well, he should have, the dancers were wearing your outfits. You must be a tiny bitty thing. The girls asked him if he minded that they borrowed a couple of your things. He replied they could have anything they wanted. Obviously, alcohol had taken over his thinking.

All of the men appeared pretty hammered. The girls had them empty the rest of the contents of their wallets into their greedy hands. Counting it up, they now had over seven hundred dollars. That bought all of the boys a trip around the world. The clothes came off one more time.

The women brought condoms with them, thank God. I was just standing back, watching the show. Each of the six remaining men took turns with each of the girls. Men really can have sex more than once in a night if they really wanted to.

When the seven hundred dollars were used up, the girls made a phone call and, a few minutes later, a car pulled up out front and the girls were gone. They left behind proof of the party.

Your house was trashed with empty beer bottles, overturned furniture and condom wrappers. Your husband excused himself from the room, and, a few minutes later, we could all hear him screaming obscenities at the top of his lungs.

I speculated that you normally do not travel with your jewelry. Your opinion is that it's always safer at home. Normally you would be correct but that night was different.

When you returned back from your trip and your husband surprised you with an upgraded wedding ring and asked you to renew your vows, I just wanted you to know why.

And you thought it was because his buddy was getting married. Your sentimental husband wanted to experience your wedding all over again. What a terrific guy!

Check the local pawn shops but keep the new ring too.

Thou Would Be Foolish To Marry Him Again,
The Other Woman

"One Mistake Can Cost"

JOURNAL

Dear Diary,

Bachelor parties are never wise. I really believe alcohol plays a huge role in adultery. When these guys get together for this festive event, they pressure each other as if its high school all over again.

"Come on Ralph, your wife will never find out!" Partially because of pressure and the rest because of not wanting to be the odd man out, they find themselves doing the deed. A moment of pleasure for a lifetime of guilt, maybe?

Can sex be bought that easily? Yes is the answer!

I am a big fan of having both the bachelor and bachelorette parties together. The bride and groom should just get all of their friends together and have a riot. Starting a marriage out with adultery can only lead to broken hearts.

The husband I was speaking of was actually a nice guy from all other accounts. Very responsible, never cheated before; even at his own bachelor party. A stupid decision which cost him Ten Thousand dollars!

Was it worth it? I'm sure it wasn't but at the time, testosterone was telling him differently!

He thought his wife would be excited with the updated proposal and new ring. I'm sure she was until the next day she opened her mailbox and received my letter.

I wonder what tomorrow will bring. I have an early flight and a conference I must attend. Good Night.

Heather

Dear Heather,

I met your husband last night.....

I was in Florida for a very boring convention. I could not believe how ridiculous some of the speakers appeared to sound.

They were so full of themselves, talking on and on without a care in the world. Do they not notice people yawning and sleeping, or do they just not care?

I was not the only one stuck in that awful conference room. I was just one of a couple hundred in forced attendance. Yes, I wrote "forced", because the attendees required this convention to finish continuing education in our field.

Doing my best to not fall asleep myself, I noticed one of the speakers had his fly down. All the way down. I started scanning the crowd to see if anyone else noticed. Yep, lots of people did. There were hushed comments spoken throughout the theater. Some people pointing, a couple really loud giggles, but not one person pointed it out to this pour sap standing on stage.

What was someone to do? Scream from the audience. "Dude! Zip Up Your Pants?" The atmosphere changed though; people appeared more interested in hearing him talk. Because of the giggles, the speaker thought he was entertaining. I guess he sorta was now.

Moving myself closer to the stage, I just had to get a better look. Red satin it looked like. He was very animated when speaking, as he waived his arms and squatted his legs; the zipper opened up even more as if he was a ventriloquist and his zipper was the real mouth.

I was just chuckling away, maybe a little too loud, and your husband noticed me. You already realized your man was the speaker. Please don't be embarrassed for him, yet.

How many times have you seen a man with his zipper down and you never said a word? It's difficult having a conversation with that person, is it not? Why do people never say anything?

I had moved upfront to get courage to say something, anything, to this husband of yours. I start pointing to his crotch and he smiled further as he kept delivering his boring lecture. I pointed again, and that time he winked. I then pointed at my own zipper, and he raised his brow. I proceeded to unzip my own zipper but he just kept speaking. His red undies now sticking out through the open fly, what once resembled an open mouth now was complete with a tongue. He moved behind the podium.

Because he moved, I thought he finally understood what I was trying to tell him. Ten minutes later, he stepped to the side once again and the mouth had returned. The tongue was gone though.

My last attempt was me zipping and unzipping my pants. Well, he stuck that tongue out again so quick, flashed me one more smile and stepped again behind the podium.

I gave up at that point. Please keep in mind that the people next to me are dying in hysteria over my show and his foolish misunderstanding of my attempt to help him.

I Met Your Husband Last Night

He ended his talk with the following words: "Thank you everyone for coming. Usually no one laughs at my jokes, so I have to say, I am pleased to see all of you think I am funny. Enjoy the rest of the conference." They thought he was humorous alright.

I endured three more hours of torture and finally the balance of the speakers finished. I grabbed my bag and laptop and off I was to the hotel bar.

Oh, how I needed a cocktail. Standing in the corner of the lounge, speaking to a couple was your husband. I am happy to report to you his zipper was up.

I settled in at the bar and while waiting for the bartender, I turned on my computer. I have been trying to work on this book I am writing, it's called "His Admission". Maybe one day you will see it in bookstores.

The bartender finally walked up and asked what I would like. I told him what I really desired was to have all the men in the world be honest with their wives. Boy, he gave me a strange look and told me he is a drink mixer, not a wish maker. He apparently did not want to switch careers, so I ordered *Sex on the Beach*. Leaving me to my writing, he disappeared.

I could see approaching out of the corner of my eye, your husband. He had attempted to slide into the chair next to me gracefully, but instead caught his foot in my briefcase strap and tripped. His face had landed in my lap and both of his hands grabbed the nearest objects, my breasts. He was stunned for a moment and just stayed in that position, and then he looked up at me.

"Hi!" was all he could muster up.

"Hello, do you think you can move for me? The law of gravity may do its own damage to my body; I really don't need your additional help. " I proceeded to undo his life lock on my twins.

"Sorry." He regained his balance and took the seat next to me. Your husband noticed previously before his interruption that, I was typing away on my keyboard. "What are you working on?"

I was a little irritated, I answered him sharply. "A book."

"Oh, that's interesting. So, you're a writer too? Are you hoping to be famous so you can quit your day job?" Your obnoxious husband really thought he was cute.

I answered really bitchy that time. "If annoying people like you keep bothering me, the only thing I will be famous for is assault and battery."

"Touchy, Touchy! Let me buy you a drink and let's start over again." With that, he signaled the bartender.

The bartender approached, already having my drink in hand, your "red underwear man" told him to put it on his tab. I stopped the bartender, swallowed my drink in full, ordered another one and requested the new one also be put on his tab.

"What are you drinking?" This guy of yours has no idea when to just shut up.

Annoyed yet again, I answered "Sex on the Beach". He was clearly amused. I waited for a comeback but he never delivered. Thankfully.

The cocktail loosened me up and I was able to relax a bit more. The thought crossed my mind I was not playing my part of The Other Woman very well tonight, so I bent over, reached into my bag and retrieved my stilettos. Switching shoes was all it took for me to have a new attitude. He only watched in awe as I slipped my sexy feet into those five-inch heels. Yet another thing he did not question.

I thanked him for the cocktails, since I neglected to do that before. He did ask what the book was about and I decided to tell him. Just as I was beginning to speak, he excused himself from our seating area to use the restroom.

As he walked away the barkeep delivered my other drink. I resumed typing and completed a couple of paragraphs before your husband returned.

He sat down again, this time without falling on me and I was greeted once more with the gaping mouth in the crotch of his pants. Geez, I thought to myself. This guy really has zipper issues. A fleeting thought crossed my mind that I should tell him, but it quickly disappeared; why should I be nice now?

"Sorry" he spoke softly. "I did not mean to interrupt you; please tell me about your book."

A waitress approached and asked him if he wanted something to drink. I never realized the bartender never bothered. Funny. He ordered a beer. I watched her eyes go to your husband's open fly; she then looked up at me, smiled and walked away.

"Are you Catholic?" I asked him.

"You're writing a book about religion?" he questioned.

As I closed my laptop I said "No, answer my question."

"Nope, why?" He had this quizzical look on his face.

I continued to tell him I was not Catholic either, but one thing that always intrigued me was the philosophy which a catholic could confess his or her sins, say one to a thousand Hail Marys, and all was forgiven. That amazes me. It's like a sin pass; do whatever you want as long as you confess and everything is OK, but what does the priest do with all of those admissions?

Before I finished telling him about the book, I sidetracked for a moment to tell him about one personal experience I had with a priest and the Catholic Church.

It was an Easter Sunday and my boyfriend, who was Catholic, wanted me to join him. I dressed in conservative clothing and we entered through the doors of the church. The first thing I noticed was this large brass fountain filled with water. I asked him what it was for. I did not notice any birds flying freely in the foyer to the cathedral and the bowl did not contain any fish. He of course laughed and said it was Holy Water. Just as he was telling me, a couple walked up, dipped their fingers in the water and applied it to their forehead in the motion of a cross. Interesting I thought.

Then the priest walked up and said hello to my boyfriend; when the priest was introduced to me, he looked at my eyes and stopped. He was frozen like a statue. My boyfriend was trying to get his attention; he must have said "Father MacDonald" three times. I felt very awkward; the priest finally came back to his senses and asked me if he could speak to me in private. Of course I had to walk away with him.

He took me to a private corner and began. "Dear Child, you must come to church more often." He visibly looked scared. He asked me if I was wearing colored contact lenses. I replied I was not.

He cupped both of my hands in his, the color from his face was draining, and he was very pale. "You have the eyes of the beast! Is the devil in your soul?" I have to admit, I was very freaked out. I loosened my hands from his grip and hurried back to my boyfriend, never answering him. As I walked back, I thought about my eyes. They are gold, Ok maybe more yellow. They are different, I admit it, but my forehead does not contain the digits 666. Could I be a demon child?

My boyfriend wanted to know what the father talked about. I agree it's one time in my life I was rendered speechless. We had taken our seats for the sermon to begin. The priest started speaking. I don't remember what he said, but he produced a bowl and some kind of wand, dripping the wand into the bowl and then zapping his audience with Holy water. All I could think was "Holy crap, don't let that stuff hit me!"

Holy Man started at one end of the room and was approaching our seating section. Yep, here it was coming. It was slow motion at the time. I could see these drops of water flying at a snail's pace in the air; sure enough, a huge drop hit my cheek. I waited for it to burn and nothing happened. I sat there stunned and relieved. My boyfriend told me I could wipe it off because it was rolling down my cheek.

I heard years later the priest had to admit himself to a detox clinic. To this day, the experience haunts me. I will never set foot in a Catholic Church again.

Your husband was amused by my story, so I went back on track with the book itself. I shared with him over the years, I have a habit of collecting admissions. I would ask mostly men to write on a slip of paper; share something they never told anyone else. These men were strangers and I would request they do not sign the paper. I collected these admissions for ten years and felt it would make an interesting publication. The priest may not be able to tell, but I could!

Your husband was very intrigued. It was extremely difficult having any type of conversation with him because I could not help but look at his lap. I decided to play with your man a bit. I wanted to see if I could make him stick his tongue out again. Yes, I know. Bad girl!

Moving off the subject of my book, I asked him if he thought my breasts were real or fake. Some of my girlfriends which had boob jobs would ask people that question. Both men and women were surveyed; more often than not, my friends would grab the individual's hands and place them on their new breasts. The question is "Do They Feel Real?"

Your husband said he was not sure. So, following in the footsteps of my friends, I placed your husband's hands on my breasts and asked him again. His hands had already been there once, but this time it was different because I did it for him. Yep, the tongue appeared. He was very keyed up. I presume nothing close to this ever happened to him before. I informed him they were indeed real.

My mission was accomplished and it was getting late. Telling him I needed to call it a night, he asked if he could give me an admission. I pulled out my scratch pad with the devil on it; he removed a pen from his shirt pocket and scratched something down. Folding the paper, he said "Good Bye" as he handed it to me.

I made my way back to my room. After settling in for the evening, I unfolded the piece of paper and it said the following.

"I get off on flashing people!"

Well, I guess he was not one of those men who just forget to zip back up, he does it on purpose!

If you stay married to him, you might want to get him pull-up pants with no zippers.

Ugh,
The Other Woman

"It Shrinks"
JOURNAL

Dear Diary,

Men are so very strange. Just another fetish!

When I was a little girl, I was actually flashed by a man. My girlfriend and I stood on a corner close to our house; we might have been ten years old. We were dancing to the music being played from this auto repair place on the corner. Separating the building and where we stood was an alley. One day, this car drove down the block and turned into the alley, and then came around the block again. Every time the car passed, it would turn into the opposite alley.

After at least five trips circling around, the car stopped in the middle of the alley. My friend and I walked over and peeked. Standing in between the door and his car, there was a man with his pants down, yanking on his penis.

We screamed and booked out of there so quick I think our tennis shoes left tread marks on the sidewalk. We went home and told our Moms who proceeded to call the police. Of course, it would have been a male police officer who showed up to take the report.

We described the vehicle and the driver and, before long, they had him under arrest. The police phoned to tell my mom that Mr. Sicko had an active warrant out for his arrest for arrears in child support. He was already going to jail.   The officer asked if we wanted to press charges. To spare my friend and me from having to go to court, our parents declined.

To this day, I think back and mull over this pervert's children. I am very happy he was not my father!

Tonight, when my eyes kept being drawn to this guy's crotch, I couldn't help but consider why that happens. As much as we try to not look, we look anyway. Is that what happens when a woman stands before a man and he is speaking to her breasts and not her face? They can't help it?

I personally find it very annoying. "Hello?" my face is up here. One day in the past and now, whenever I am in the mood, I do the following...

If some guy is staring at my chest and talking to it instead of my face, I start staring at their groin and holding my conversation with it. After a few moments, they realize I am not moving my eyes up. It's comical to see how uncomfortable they actually get. Sometimes they will then sit down but, to prove a point, I still keep looking and talking to their penis. You know how it's said the cold will cause them to shrink. Try this exercise, it has the same effect!

I get to fly home tomorrow, yippee. Traveling is fun but I miss the comfort of my own bed.

Good Night!

Christy

Dear Christy,

I met your husband last night.....

I was out of town for a work related conference and was extremely happy to come home. I traveled to the airport to catch my red eye flight.

I never fly lightly; I always have over packed bags. You never know when you may need different things. My three suitcases stood in line at security with me. Let me tell you the line was long and the area did not smell very good. Ever since the September 11th tragedies, the airports have beefed up their security measures. Removing your shoes is now a requirement of all passengers.

The metal detector must not come all the way to the floor, right? Why not install a floor mat which screens everyone's feet? They do not have you remove your socks. Wouldn't someone just keep whatever they are hiding inside their socks on the soles of their feet? A floor mat screening device would eliminate that problem; I guess *Home Land Security* has yet to figure it out. My idea would also spare the passengers and security personnel the terrible odor radiating from the area. Gosh, does it smell bad!

Finally, it had been my turn to go through the x-ray doorway. Of course, it had to beep. They had me step back and go through again. Once more, it signaled security I had something metal on me. Removing my belt and jewelry, it happened for the third time. I finally figured out maybe my belly button ring was causing the commotion. Lifting my shirt for the officer, he smiled and sent me over to a boxed-in area. Another officer brought my three bags with him.

Lifting my arms, they "wand" me. With that part being finished, they start ruffling through my bags. I had toys with me. The guy handling the search picks up my vibrator and looked back at me. Was I embarrassed? No. If men did a better job satisfying us women, we would not have to have imitation dicks. They are the ones who should be embarrassed.

He turned it on. You know the sound it makes, everyone within earshot glanced over. The men appeared surprised and several women gave me the thumbs-up. I was informed that it could be used as a weapon and security needed to keep it. Are you kidding me? What was I going to do, break into the pilot's cabin, have the pilot bend over and stick it up his butt and force him to fly the plane to my choice of destination? A weapon, seriously! Every man wonders what it would feel like, which is why strap on's are popular. It couldn't be a weapon. Auh, unless the pilot was a woman, then, yes, it could be. I argued no further and was released to my flight.

I finally made it to my gate as they were announcing the final boarding call. Passing through the checkpoint without any issues, I walked into the plane. The pilot and co-pilot had been greeting everyone who boarded. I couldn't help but imagine them with my vibrator stuck up their butts. Grinning to myself, I said hello and made my way to my seat.

Everyone on the plane looked as tired as I felt. The redeye is a perfect flight because you can sleep throughout it and, in the blink of an eye you have arrived at your final stop.

I placed my bags in the overhead and squeezed into my row. I had the window seat and your husband was seated in the aisle. The stewards closed the door which meant your husband and I did not have a middle passenger. Good. Room to lounge!

As I was getting situated, your man said Hello to me. I smiled and continued to try and locate the safety belt. I was sitting on one part of it and he kindly helped me. His hands glided under my butt and he pulled it loose. I thanked him.

I want to give you my first impression of your husband. He was a cute guy, not overly handsome, not ugly, appearing attractive and pleasant to look at. His eyes sparkled like little stars; he had the aura of a little boy. Of course, his height added to the element. He was a little guy. Even though I did not see him standing, you could still tell while he was in a sitting position. He was certainly smaller than me.

The plane was taxing down the runway and the flight crew started their broadcast of emergency instructions. I am always humored when they talk about the safety floatation devices on flights which will not be traveling over any bodies of water. Like this one. But, just in case the plane falls from the sky and I am lucky enough to fall into someone's pool, I know I won't drown!

Once the plane reached whatever altitude it needed to be at, the crew began serving refreshments. I was looking for a cocktail. Just a little something to mimic a sleeping pill! It would help me relax and hopefully dose off.

I can't stand when my ears start popping in the air. I looked over and up an aisle and noticed a pregnant woman. What happens to the baby with the altitude? Do its ears pop too, or is that how Meconium (baby poop) gets released into the womb?

The pressure of air flight can make you have gas; I would think it could make a baby poop. I wonder if a study was ever done on that. My thoughts were interrupted by your husband speaking to me.

"I'm sorry, can you repeat that? My ears are plugged." I replied as I was tugging on my ear lobes.

"Would you like a pillow and blanket?" he had asked.

"Yes, that would be great!" At least the flight would be more comfortable.

He had signaled to a flight attendant, she approached and he made his request.

Odd thoughts are always passing through my head. The stewardess was an attractive lady but older, fifty or so. Most fifty-year olds are not as well put together as her. When I was little, I always wanted to be a flight attendant. It ranked right up there with model and Professional Football Cheerleader. The impression left with me since childhood was these ladies are model types. However, most of the flights I have taken in recent years have only older women or gay men working them. What happened? Are these older women, the hot young things which worked when I was little, aged? Have the airlines finally quit discriminating? Why are there so many gay men working flights now? Is it because straight people do not know how to have fun anymore and the airlines are hiring to suit their customer base of gay passengers who travel? Or did the wives of the heads of the airlines get together and tell their husbands they were tired of them having affairs with the crew and now they can only hire older women and gay men? If that is the case, these wives failed to realize these cougars are probably more dangerous than their counterpart cubs. And some of their husbands are bisexual.

Bringing me back once more from analyze land, your husband handed me my sleeping gear. The beverage cart was now at our aisle and I requested vodka and orange juice. Your man followed my lead and requested the same, in addition requesting her to double each of our orders. He paid with cash for both of us. I really can't remember the last time I ever bought a cocktail for myself.

We toasted and slammed down our first drink. We continued to converse about all sorts of stupid stuff. I ended up telling him about my experience with security. He laughed and told me you have a collection of bedside toys. Good for you girl!

After finishing our second round, he ordered two more for each of us. Getting hammered on our flight was fun!

The plane traveled through some airspace which caused us to start jumping around a little. Turbulence. I really hate flying. Your husband noticed and he moved into the middle seat, putting his arm around me. He told me to not be scared; to think of driving on a bumpy road. That's all fine and dandy, but if this plane was a car, it would only bump to a shoulder of the road; this giant people vessel in the air could fall from the sky.

The pilot announced he was climbing to a higher altitude. I glanced over to the pregnant woman and noticed her grab her belly. Ok, maybe babies won't poop but can her stomach bust? Pop like a balloon. She looked miserable. Men have such an easy life. I could see her mouth moving. If I could read lips, I imagine she was cursing out the bastard who did this to her.

As our drinks arrived, the plane leveled off in space without any further potholes.

Feeling very buzzed, I lifted my blanket and placed it over your husband and me. He was very comforting and I wanted to make sure he was not going to leave my side.

I asked him if he liked touching. He was a little surprised by the question and wanted to know what I meant. "Touching, you know foreplay?"

"Of course!", he replied as he moved over a tad closer to me.

I wanted to know if he still touched you. My personal feeling is once the hot and heavy is out of the relationship, couples do not touch each other enough anymore. When they have sex, the man is looking to be stroked but he neglects to touch his wife. Women like to be petted too.

He admitted he does not touch you like he did in the beginning. He appeared to be embarrassed by his confession.

I proceeded to ask him if he wanted to practice on me. He was thrilled and accepted my invitation. The plane was very quiet; many of the fellow passengers were sleeping. The flight crew disappeared to the back of the plane and most of the lights were off.

He slipped his hand under our blanket and unbuttoned the first button of my jeans. I was getting very warm and moist. I was reminded of being much younger and on a first date.

I had button-fly jeans on. Each one he unfastened had my heart beating a little quicker. He traced me with his fingers starting at my belly button over my clothing and down to my groin. Hot, hot, hot! I couldn't wait for him to slip his hand inside my panties.

Satisfied that he had me very aroused, he slid my jeans down on my hips. Leaving my g-string in place, he fooled around on the outside first. I was saturated.

Taking his hand, he now effortlessly entered the top of my undies and slide all the way down until he reached the small lake I created. The wetness allowed his fingers to glide back and forth across me. Wow, it felt incredible!

Using one of his fingers he entered me. I opened my legs a little further to give him easier access then he used two and three fingers. I do believe its girth not length that counts. Well, that's if he is at least six inches.

When he would withdraw, he would flick his fingers at my be-be, then rub harder in that spot. I couldn't take it anymore and I quivered in desire.

Isn't it amusing that after an orgasm, we are so sensitive we can't be touched anymore?

Without me even touching him, he had released himself. We were both sitting there, sticky and satisfied. He told me he had forgotten what it was like and said he was going to be a little different with you from now on. Foreplay is a good word and a great action.

Although I never did get any sleep, I had an enjoyable flight. When we finally landed, your husband turned to me and offered the following statement:

"I have failed as a man. If my wife uses those battery operated toys in the nightstand without me, I have not been doing my job. I promise to take care of her better so the object she feels inside of her has blood going through it instead of wires."

With that, we parted ways. Keep this letter as a reminder to him of the commitment he made. Don't get rid of the toys yet.

Sparing You from Having To Buy Batteries; Hopefully,
The Other Woman

"The "O"

JOURNAL

Dear Diary,

I am happy to report I am at home once again.

After my little fun with my fellow passenger, I thought of something.

Multiple orgasms!

I have heard about them. I have read about them. I have been told about them.

I have never had one.

I don't understand how it is even remotely possible. Once my body has had one, I am so sensitive and numb. Until the swelling goes down, nothing else is going to happen for a while.

Sure, I can have multiple orgasms in a day but not in succession like fireworks. Am I built differently or are those other women out of their minds? Myth?

Maybe I have just never been with the right man. Yes, easier to blame them instead of me, right? I guess I will just have to keep trying until I accomplish that goal, then I will proudly sport a t-shirt that says...

"I have had multiples O's and I'm not lying".

Why do women lie to men about having one at all? There's an actress in each of us. "Oh, yeah, Baby, almost, right there, auhhhhhh. That was perfect!"

Do these men not appreciate its extremely difficult for us anyway? We have to block out all of the sounds, quit thinking about the kids, angle our bodies just the right way and continuously keep hitting our favorite spot all without suffering leg cramps.

How about when we are almost there and he's done. He rolls over or just lays still and exhales a deep breath. "That was great honey!" And we girls are thinking... "Hello?! It was Ok until you stopped." When I was married and that happened, I would roll over, grab his hand, place it down there and tell him to make me cum. I didn't go through all of that exercise for nothing. I would make him finish the job!

Good Bye for Now!

A day of rest on the water is the plan for tomorrow.

Jillian

Dear Jillian,

I met your husband last night.....

Have you ever noticed how many times people remarry? I have friends who have been married two, three and some four times.

You would think they would have learned their lesson after the first time.

It's difficult to find someone later in life that has never been married. The picking pool is usually recycled ex-husbands. Come on, if someone else divorced them, why does the new woman think it's going to be any different for them?

I also have a couple of friends who lived with their lovers. Everything was great! Cupid flew down one day, struck the couple in the heart and after fifteen years, they marry.

Within six months the newlyweds are heading to divorce court.

What's up with that piece of paper? My intelligence tells me it may be a contract with the devil. You sign the license and you are doomed to hell! You agree, don't you? If not, you will when you are done reading my letter.

It was the weekend again and I was so looking forward to taking out my boat.

I Met Your Husband Last Night

Coasting several miles away from shore, I found my familiar hidden cove, known as Partier Paradise. Usually, several hundred boats are in attendance. Everyone ties their vessels together; it reminds me of a floating city.

Everyone becomes a family. You can just walk from boat to boat and have cocktails and conversation. Sometimes even more!

The water out in the hideaway is crystal clear; there also is a warm spring which feeds through the lake area. Naked bodies swim and play with each other.

With gas prices being so high, this is a perfect solution to conserve fuel expenses. Of course, some of the boats are so big; it still costs the owners a couple of hundred bucks to reach their desired destination. But it's so worth it!

My boat is named "The Other Woman". It is a fitting name. Have you ever noticed most boats are named after women? I have often considered why that is so. Is it because they are expensive, just like us? Or it is because men feel we can be controlled and owned?

That day on the lake did not appear to be any different then days previous. That was, until I saw your husband.

He was hanging out with a bunch of his buddies. You were nowhere around. I guess he did not invite you to come out and play. Maybe you were stuck at home with the kids. Sucks sometimes, doesn't it?

When I pulled my boat in, I was easily able to tie up to his. Yours was one of those really big boats; it could hold about twenty-five people comfortably. Someone must have a great job.

Saving One Wife At A Time

201 -

I Met Your Husband Last Night

I am a true believer in fate. Your watercraft actually has my name on it! It was almost like a big flashing sign calling and pulling me to your husband; my very own personal welcoming mat.

After tying up, one of the other guys asked me to hop over to your boat. He was holding a cocktail in his hand and a warm inviting smile, his naked tan chest glistening in the sun.

How could I resist? Once I boarded, I watched your husband chase some other girl around your boat. He kept snapping a wet towel at her. Red marks streaked her nude bottom.

All of the girls were topless, even the ones who should not have been. They must not own mirrors, I decided.

Although your vessel and those surrounding contained many handsome males, I was captivated by your sultry husband.

He had finally caught the girl he was chasing. He tackled her on one of the benches and began applying suntan oil all over her already bronzed skin. I found it very erotic to watch him touching her. It reminded me of times which I was the recipient of such pleasure.

Fleeting memories of my past swirled around my mind. I had met my husband out on this lake many, many years ago. Isn't it funny how we never forget those we loved? No matter how hard we try or how bad they broke our heart?

Enough of the sad stuff, we can't live in the past right? So I will continue my story about your husband.

I decided I wanted to feel his hands on me. I walked away from the cute guy and strolled right over to yours.

I sat right down on the lap of a girl he was rubbing down. I asked her to undo my bikini top, invisibly patting myself on the back for my great idea to get your husband's motor started.

His girl toy had already consumed enough alcohol which, if lit, she could have been a human bonfire. She was more than happy to play along.

After she untied the strings, she pulled the straps down and peeled away my suit. When my beach balls were fully exposed, she wrapped her arms around me and extended her hands to touch me. Someone handed her the oil and she rubbed me down.

We had an audience. Your husband enjoyed watching. After our little production, I pulled him over to me and removed his *Speedos*. The oil had allowed me to easily slide my hands up and down his mast.

He finally could not take it anymore. He swept me up in his arms and carried me to the belly of his boat. There was a beautiful bed in there. The sheets were made of silk which allowed our hot skin to cool a little.

The other girl hooked up with one of your man's buddies', she didn't seem to mind. It turned out she was your husband's girlfriend; she had been pretty drunk and did not even notice us going into the cabin. A word of wisdom: Always know where your man is!

I explored his whole body and he mine. Touching and tasting each other reminded me of a feast. He was hungry and I was famished for his attention.

I was having a great time! Our love session had familiarity to it. I was comfortable and satisfied. I performed my favorite acrobats and we each satisfied our fetishes together.

Please consider this letter as my late wedding gift to you. You might want to change the name of the boat. Otherwise, I will always consider it to be an invitation.

Once a dog, always a dog! You couldn't possibly think you were special?

Oh, by the way, I always wanted to say "Thank You" for opening my eyes.

Congratulations,
The Other Woman

"Once A Dog, Always A Dog"

JOURNAL

Dear Diary,

It had been a long time since I have seen my ex-husband. I guess I will always feel something for him. I really can't say I miss much; other than the sex.

My parents were divorced when I was a little girl. Although my dad remarried, he still carried on sexually with my mom for years. I think the last time they got it on was 15 years after they separated. My guess is most of the new wives have no idea their new husbands still smell their way home again.

I wonder if this means that, in another ten years, I will be screwing my ex-husband again.

How can these new wives think their cheating husbands are going to be faithful to them? Stupid Chicks!

A word of wisdom... If you are going to marry someone who has been divorced because of adultery in the marriage, make sure you hook up with the guy whose wife screwed around on *him!*

As far as paybacks to the new wife; No, I was only giving her back the present she gave to me. Truth and Life!

Exhausted from all the play, Good Night.

Dear Reader,

Are my stories farfetched? I will tell you no. Although this book is labeled fiction, it contains more truth than not. No, I personally have not run around and had affairs with these men, but I have met them and they did share their stories. To protect the innocent, if you can call them that, their admissions have been modified. Men and women have secrets, desires and fetishes. You never know what happens behind closed doors, unless you ask, catch them or they tell you on their own.

After twenty years of being in a male dominated industry, I have met too many married men and have thought about each one of their wives. I would never mail a letter or rat on them, it's not my place BUT, this book did bring me some satisfaction.

Waking each day allows all of us to have a new start at life. To strive for happiness in every area. Relationships require special care, but the work has to come from both parties.

The next page explains the number one (my opinion) problem we experience in dating or marriages. It is a flaw women are born with and a major difference between the two sexes. Read it, agree or not. My favorite line is the last one. I hang my hat on that statement alone.

The Other Woman was created to help out unsuspecting wives. My final gift for those who have nothing to save is a preprinted letter to give to your husband. It may be a tad cruel but "All Is Fair in Love and War" (John Lyly's 'Euphues' 1578).

xoxo
The Other Woman

"The Grudge Factor"

Final note from the Author....

I have always thought that our brains resemble filing cabinets. We keep collecting information around us every day and then file it away. When a drawer gets overloaded, we either empty it, shuffle some stuff around or we just don't retain anything new.

Some individuals, men and women, choose to fill their files with useless information, I, on the other hand, suck at trivia and fill mine with what I deem important.

One drawer all ladies have in common is the "Memory of Our Men". We hold memories far too long! I personally feel we are born with this drawer space already labeled in big bright red letters. Whereas men are born <u>without</u> a "Memory of Our Women" drawer. Nor do they make one after birth.

We seem to hold onto the stupidest things in these heads of ours. We can recite dates, times and places of events or episodes which pissed us off from years previous. Then, when we finally thought we had forgotten, something starts to tickle us, a commercial, a movie, a book, a conversation and, BAM, the memory returns and we are just as pissed off as when it first happened.

Then the famous question from our men. "What's wrong?" Yep, we just did a 180 degree turn and they sensed it. "What do you mean what's wrong?" "You're an asshole, that's what's wrong!"

"I didn't do anything!"

"Yes you did, three years ago on the 12th of April at 6:02p.m.!"

Is it really fair we do this to them? Even as we're being bitches, we know that how we are acting is wrong but our anger wins over the war of logic. Men should just let us be and this also will soon pass. Maybe.

This theory of mine is a key ingredient in ruining many relationships. Women truly need to get over things and move beyond. Forgive, "Yes", but we can never forget. It's a common problem with all women around the globe.

We may need some kind of therapy or pill to help us with this issue.

Of course, if we look at it the other way...*if men did not do such stupid stuff, we wouldn't have any grudges to hold!*

xoxo
The Other Woman
April de Cardenas

PS: If you see my husband cheating on me, send me a letter!

Visit me and drop me at note at
http://www.imetyourhusbandlastnight.com

SCORNED WIFE, PLEASE FEEL FREE TO USE THE FOLLOWING FORM LETTER
Please insert one or more choices on the blank line.

Dear Husband,

I have finally come to my senses and have realized you're such a

_____.

(Asshole, idiot, moron, imbecile, jerk) I want you to know I have faked _____ (one, one hundred, all) of my orgasms with you. I have not found you attractive in_____ (one year, five years, ten years, well ever). I only married you because _____ (I felt sorry for you, I was drunk, I was paid by your parents, I had a head injury). The time has come for us to part ways and let me say _____ (Thank God it's finally over, I will not miss you or your gas, maybe now I can have some fun and the big "O", I will enjoy clicker control and the absence of your presence.) I was contacted by The Other Woman and she told me that _____ (You're a sick *uck, you're inbred, camels have better humps then you). She has helped me open my eyes that _____ (life will be much better without you, you have only worn me down and you suck in bed, I need to get laid by a real man). I am leaving you with this _____ (A-HA! Nothing! I have taken it all, my attorney bill, the kids, your mother and/or all of the above). Maybe in the future you will _____ (keep your dick in your pants, remember to tell your wife yourself, have the next wife sign a pre-nup or all of the above.)

Hating You from the Bottom of My Being,

Your Soon To Be Ex-Wife_____
(your name here)

Porno

PLEASE FEEL FREE TO USE THE FOLLOWING FORM LETTER

Dear Husband,

I went through your history on the computer and noticed you have spent an incredible amount of time surfing pornography websites, while in care of our children and when I was at work.

After calculating the time just in the past week, it appears you have a major problem. Your issues are not solely with your sick perversion, but you have also ruined our keyboard by adding a sticky substance that is a foreign matter to our computer.

I have downloaded your content and plan on producing it as evidence in our divorce trial.

I never knew you had such a love for farm animals. Maybe that explains why in the middle of the night you make sounds which resemble those of a sheep.

Anyway, I am happy to know that, in your miserable life, you have finally accomplished something. Not everyone can lose their kids, wife, house and pension by key-stroking. You deserve the "All American Stupid Perv" award. Your children and parents will be proud.

The process server is looking for you. Now get the *uck out of my house.

Love Always,

PRE MARITIAL CHECKLIST
"Saving You From Divorce"

- ☐ Wife will continue shopping.
- ☐ Wife will continue to have nails done.
- ☐ Wife will continue to go tanning.
- ☐ Wife will continue to go to the Hair Salon.
- ☐ Wife will continue to have massages.
- ☐ Husband will continue to have massages.
- ☐ Wife will continue to go to the Gym
- ☐ Husband will continue to go to the Gym.
- ☐ Daily Outing With The Girls.
- ☐ Twice Weekly Outings With Girls.
- ☐ Weekly Outings With Girls.
- ☐ Bi-Weekly Outing With Girls.
- ☐ Monthly Outing With Girls.
- ☐ Girls Only Weekends Away
- ☐ Daily Outing With The Guys.
- ☐ Twice Weekly Outings With Guys.
- ☐ Weekly Outings With Guys.
- ☐ Bi-Weekly Outing With Guys.
- ☐ Monthly Outing With Guys.
- ☐ Guys Only Weekends Away.
- ☐ Sex with each other _____ Weekly
- ☐ Husband will travel south on wife _____ daily, weekly, monthly, yearly
- ☐ Wife will perform Lolly Pop on husband _____ daily, weekly, monthly, yearly
- ☐ Wife will have _____ money per week to spend on nothing.
- ☐ Husband will have _____ money per week to spend on nothing.
- ☐ We will have my own bank accounts.
- ☐ We will have a joint bank account.
- ☐ Wife will pay the following bills only_____
- ☐ We will jointly split all bills.
- ☐ Wife will handle writing out all of the bills.
- ☐ Husband will handle writing out all of the bills.
- ☐ We will meet weekly and do the bills together.
- ☐ We want animals such as a _____
- ☐ We never want animals
- ☐ We _____ number of children
- ☐ We want to start having babies _____ years into our marriage
- ☐ We never want to have children
- ☐ We agree to name our son after you
- ☐ We will never name our son after you
- ☐ Wife weighs this weight now _____ and could weigh as much as _____
- ☐ Husband weighs this weight now _____ and could weigh as much as _____
- ☐ Husband likes your mother
- ☐ Wife likes your mother
- ☐ Wife will wash your clothes
- ☐ Husband will wash your clothes

Please Share! A Larger Copy Is Available At
www.imetyourhusbandlastnight.com

MERCHANDISE STORE

CHEATER
LIVES HERE

"CHEATER LIVES HERE LAWN SIGNS"

T-Shirts

HER HUSBANDS
BABY
INSIDE

Please visit www.imetyourhusbandlastnight.com

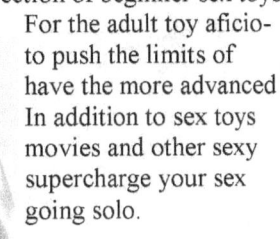

About Photographer: John Bailey

Since childhood John Bailey has always been a creative talent. His path, both professionally and personally, has led him into a world immersed in the visual arts.

By trade John is a Freelance Promo Producer in the New York City area. Over the past decade he has worked on projects for various media outlets including The Sci Fi Channel, USA Network, Sleuth, Universal HD and MTV Networks. He has written and produced numerous broadcast promotional commercials for various programs including *Stargate Universe, Stargate SG-1, Stargate Atlantis, Battlestar Galactica, Ghost Hunters, Who Wants To Be A Superhero?, The Dead Zone*, as well as many others.

John has taken his vast knowledge of video production, 3D animation and special effects work, and applied it to several personal projects including his self-produced and directed short film *Shadow Kill*, as well as the forthcoming sequel webisode series. He has produced and directed two music videos for international singing sensation Laureta Meci. Also an accomplished photographer, John creates images that uniquely blend real life photography as well as 3D special effects elements.

John would like to thank April de Cardenas for this wonderful opportunity to be a part of a truly special book, which he hopes every reader will enjoy! John would also like to thank his family, friends, and colleagues for all their support and encouragement.

Please take a moment to explore John Bailey's work on the following websites:

www.shadowkill.tv

www.modelmayhem.com/JohnBaileyPictures

www.lauretameci.com

www.myspace.com/johnbaileyfilms